WRONG PLACE

TIME

Tom Stearns

Also by Tom Stearns

Personal Demons

The Cleaner

Earth View

The Finder

Jenna

With thanks to C.A. Viruet.

Contents

CHAPTER ONE 5

CHAPTER TWO 18

CHAPTER THREE 29

CHAPTER FOUR 51

SIMON 69

CHAPTER SIX 74

CHAPTER SEVEN 85

CHAPTER EIGHT 92

MARC 100

CHAPTER TEN 117

CHAPTER ELEVEN 136

CHAPTER TWELVE 152

CHAPTER THIRTEEN 165

CHAPTER FOURTEEN 181

CHAPTER FIFTEEN 193

CHAPTER SIXTEEN 205

AUTHOR'S NOTE 210

CHAPTER ONE

Her husband had bled out after five minutes. The Spotty one had gutted George with a cool efficiency that suggested it was the latest in a long list. The cut was so ruthless George struggled to keep his intestines from spilling to the floor. Even in her shocked state, Fey couldn't tell if his horrified expression was due to staining the plush, golden carpet fitted a week earlier or the realisation he was about to die.

She had looked into her husband's eyes, tried to reassure him, comfort him until the skinny one finished the job by slicing the love of her life's throat.

Fey was glad her husband of twenty years had so easily died. It spared him witnessing the obscene things they had done to her.

They'd abused her for hours. They carved things on her and pushed things into her, brutalised every inch of her, attacked everything private and made it theirs. They reduced her to nothing but flesh. Her husband got off lightly; when they pushed the ornaments from the mantelpiece into him he was already dead. Death spared him the pain of them slicing his penis from his body and the horror of watching them force her to suck the dead organ. The bastards had almost pissed themselves laughing they found it so funny.

Her husband's penis was still inside her somewhere. She had no sensation in her genitals now, other than burning fire. Her anus wept a solid stream of blood.

When bored with their torture, they decided it was time to gratify themselves physically.

Spotty went first, and it had been over quickly. He drooled on her as he came and tried to make her look at him. She knew to obey or he would hurt her, she just couldn't do it. She only opened her eyes after he'd broken her jaw.

The Skinny one was unable to finish and had become enraged. She'd debased herself by trying to help

him along with her muscles. Her efforts to shorten her ordeal stung her both physically and emotionally as it felt like compliance. Skinny had noticed her attempts to grip him and stomped on her ribs as a reward. She went away then. She had no idea where.

She awoke to the Skinny one urinating on her face. His piss stung her eyes. As it washed over her face, she tasted semen. Skinny had gotten himself off after all.

Spotty and Skinny hadn't killed her. There was no fun in that. Why put a wounded animal out of its misery when it can suffer on for years? Spotty had said something along those lines to her. She couldn't remember the words but the gist was clear. Skinny was nervous at the idea of leaving a witness and they bickered.

Spotty put Skinny in his place.

Spotty bent down to Fey and grabbed hold of her vagina. She hadn't even bothered closing her legs or covering herself. Very early on her attackers had punished such unauthorised movements with the vilest of pains.

'See this cunt?' he said. He didn't wait for a response. 'This shitty cunt is mine. I can use it any time I fucking well want. Understand. Keep it clean and tidy. If it's a mess when I come back it'll be bad for you.' He

finished with a playful pat of her privates as if praising an obedient puppy.

Then they walked out as calmly as if they had dropped by for afternoon tea.

Fey turned to look at her husband. Skinny had arranged his body face down on his knees. Fey saw the edge of the TV remote control sticking out his rectum. Something inside her snapped, and she laughed. Her ribs protested, reducing her laughter into a moan of agony. How many ribs were broken? One? Two? It felt like all of them. Everything hurt. She was broken.

If they had left the knives, she would have slit her wrists. Her wounds may heal, but she would not put herself through telling another soul what had happened to her and her husband that day.

Fey crawled over to her husband, the movement rewarding her with fresh jolts of agony that left her breathless. Somehow she managed to get herself to a sitting position. Spots danced in front of her eyes and she almost passed out.

She pulled the TV remote from her husband. She'd known him for fifteen years and he hadn't allowed her to even put a finger up there, not even during their

most passionate of lovemaking. 'One way traffic, love,' he'd told her. To his credit, he had never asked her to do it either. She smiled at the memory of him and her lip drooled fresh blood. Her attempts and pulling his trousers up met with failure. She was in too much pain. 'Sorry, love,' she said.

She froze. The door opened. They'd changed their minds. They had come back. She prayed they'd come to kill her and not for more of the same.

'We were only joking, love,' said the spotty one. 'How could we leave a sexy bitch like you behind all alone?'

Fey saw the erections straining at both their trousers.

'Please. Don't.' Her voice so low she was sure they wouldn't hear it.

'But you're too sexy,' said Spotty.

'Let me die.'

Marc flipped her over, spat on his fingers and jabbed them into her rectum.

'All in good time, lover.'

* * *

'We've made a real mess of her,' said Simon.

'You mean *you* did.'

'I got carried away, didn't I?'

'A bit more than that.' His friend's ferocity sometimes concerned Marc. As usual, he had sliced off the woman's nipples and placed them over her dead eyes. A psychologist would have a field day with that one. They would think it showed maternal hatred, an attack on femininity, or a display of guilt. Truth was, Simon found it hilarious. The first time he'd done it he'd pissed himself laughing. 'Look, she's got nips for eyes,' he blurted between breathless giggles. His latest idea involved cutting out the vagina to take it on the road. All his attempts were unsuccessful. Far from removing the object of his desire, he destroyed the body. It wasn't like he needed the fucking thing, anyway. If they came across someone they liked they took them. Marc suspected Simon was mental.

'Forget about it,' said Marc, picking at his acne. 'You check upstairs. I'll do downstairs.'

They searched for cash and valuables. Nothing big; just jewellery, phones, and other pocket-sized items.

They hauled two Samsung phones, an iPad, thirty-eight pounds in cash and their wedding rings.

'Shit. No good.'

Marc held up the rings to Simon. Simon squinted to read the names and dates stamped on the inside.

'Bollocks,' he said and kicked Fey.

'Let's bounce,' said Marc.

* * *

Marc sensed Simon seething. Marc usually did the driving, but he was knackered. Simon hated to drive. Simon was such a wanker sometimes. He was always moaning that Marc thought he was the boss of him -- doing all the driving, telling him what to do. In a way, he was correct. Marc had lost count of how many times he had explained the way things worked or had to talk Simon out of some insanity. Simon was nowhere near as smart or as capable as he thought he was. To allow Simon to take charge would be madness and they'd be in a cell quicker

than they could blink. He was a dangerous fucker though, and Marc made sure he never pushed his luck.

Simon was sex mad for as long as Marc could remember and, even with all the fucking they were doing, it showed no signs of abating. As a teenager Simon had little luck with the girls. They were instinctively creeped out by him. It wasn't just that he was ugly, and he was certainly ugly, it was that he had no clue how to act around them and in most cases the girls ran a mile. Simon did not understand the way things worked socially, the games you had to play to get what you wanted. If he took a shine to a girl, he'd paw and rub himself up against her like a dog with two dicks. Any girls daft, drunk or desperate enough to let him have a go soon discovered he was a freak of the first order and far too rough. Marc intervened occasionally. Not because of what he was doing was wrong, but because you didn't do that to people who knew who you were.

Marc had been taking what he wanted from women he didn't know for a few years. It had left him unfulfilled. Raping joggers in the early mornings was not ideal. It was cold, and you had to be quick because some of those bitches ran like the wind. Hit them hard and fast.

You had to fuck them quick, too. There was never time to savour them. January was the best time to catch them. All those fat bitches waddling through the woods, getting their cunts all sweaty and ready for him. But dragging those fat heffers into a secluded area robbed him of his energy sometimes. Another problem with the January joggers was they preferred to waddle in pairs. That was what gave him the idea to hunt with a partner himself.

Marc had tempted Simon on his excursions with the promise of satisfying his nasty little libido. If, and it was a big if, he understood that he wasn't in charge. If it was left to Simon he'd just grab anyone he fancied off the middle of the street and fuck them in an alley.

Now there was two of them they could subdue their victims, make them do the things they wanted to do and take their time. At first Simon was satisfied, or at least said he had been. Marc could tell there was something behind the words to suggest it wasn't so. Simon was no longer content with shooting his load. Simon wanted to hurt people. If Marc was honest, he enjoyed hurting them too. When he was fucking them he punched them. He used to like them dazed. He enjoyed watching their heads lolling, eyes unfocused, while he fucked them. They knew

13

he was up inside them taking what he wanted but were too out of it to truly know or try to stop him. But the fear was king. When you had them pinned and their eyes were wide and teary and they knew, just *knew*, you were going to fuck them and there wasn't a damn thing they could do about it. *That* was the best. Now he had Simon he could do that more often. Fucking someone while they were out cold wasn't the same, they needed to be aware and powerless. Although he did like the idea of a woman waking up in the woods only to find out some bastard had used her cunt without her say so. It was a buzz.

Things changed the first time he let Simon do it alone. Marc was the one who normally made the pick as Simon was too distracted by the pussy to look at the bigger picture. Or so Marc thought.

After weeks of whining and nagging Marc had allowed Simon to pick one all for himself. Marc had helped kidnap the girl and drove them to the woods. Marc stayed in the car with the radio turned up. She was too skinny for him, her arse hardly filling her jeggings. Maybe seventeen or eighteen. Whatever age she was, there was little of her left when Simon asked him to help bury her. Every inch of her naked body was covered in bruises. Her

face was a bloody mess and her teeth and skull were exposed. He had sliced through her breasts and stuffed leaves and grass in the wounds. A bundle of twigs stuck out from between her legs.

Marc knew then he'd aligned himself with a certifiable nutter. They were tied. If Simon was caught, so was he and they'd throw away the key. Rape was rape. But this...

Over time, Marc had come to Simon's way of thinking. Not all the way, he wasn't a total psycho. He would never admit it to Simon, but Simon had helped Marc realise his inner desires. The fucking was a bonus, not the intent. His intent all along had been to devour their fear, to take what he wanted. And he hadn't been doing it properly. Simon taught him to degrade and defile. Simon was a natural.

And that made Simon dangerous. You could wind him up and let him go. Like that time in Pontefract. Jesus, he went berserk and killed the pets and everything. He'd allowed Simon's slaughter of the pets to slide for fear of getting on the wrong end of him. Not that he would ever admit it. He was the boss and Simon was wise to remember it. Problem was Simon scared Marc sometimes.

He possessed the strength and conviction of a retard when he put his mind to it.

As they left the house that morning Marc had sensed an imminent strop from Simon and thought by allowing his partner to drive it would make him feel more involved. It had helped up to a point. Simon would always feel hard done to and nothing he did would ever change that.

'You awake,' Simon asked.

'Yeah.'

'I wanna fuck a redhead. One with ginger pubes.'

Marc was relieved. If he could get Simon what he wanted, then maybe they could avoid a confrontation. 'Well, keep an eye out for one then. I'll sit it out, my fucking bell end is killing me.'

'So, she's all mine?'

'All yours.'

'Fucking brilliant.'

'Now let me get some kip.'

CHAPTER TWO

The journey was going better than expected.
Realistically Martin would be the first to admit that four
middle-aged people and two dogs stuck in a car for two
hundred miles was sure to be problematic. So far even the
roads had been kind.

'Can we stop?' asked Anne from the back seat. He
had spoken too soon.

Martin turned to his wife and found the grimace
he was dreading. She was still beautiful with her jet-black
hair and her even darker eyes. But without a smile she
looked ill. Then she always looked ill to Martin ever since
she dropped to a size ten. He had fallen for a curvaceous
size eighteen way back when. It had been over a year since
she had shed the weight and it still sometimes caught him
off guard. 'Not just yet, love.' Again, he was shocked at

17

how thin she was. No, not thin, lean. Martin was all too aware of his ample paunch as the seatbelt cut into it.

Martin turned to Keith, the poor sod who had offered to drive them all. Keith was a trim fifty-year-old with grey hair spiked into a style that should have looked ridiculous, but he somehow owned. No pot belly for Keith, mused Martin. With a wife like Marilyn it was hardly surprising. Marilyn would have warned her husband of any approaching weight gain, of that Martin had no doubt. He experienced a pang of jealousy toward his friend, not for the woman he was married to (although he wouldn't have said no to a roll in the hay if it were offered -- hypothetically of course) but for the relationship they had, the dynamic.

Keith was a stickler for journey's going to plan. It was his daily job to be on the road. The journey to Langflorn was estimated at three and a half hours and Keith had informed them earlier that he had factored in forty-five minutes for refreshment breaks. An hour and fifteen minutes in and they had already stopped for Anne to use the toilet. Everyone knew of Anne's 'situation' (as it was referred to) and allowances had been made. Martin

sometimes, unkindly, thought she was making a meal of it. He wasn't proud of thinking it. He thought it all the same.

'Can we stop please again, Martin?' Her voice was low, almost a whisper as if she was hoping her fellow passengers wouldn't hear.

'I don't even know where the next service station is,' he replied.

Keith tapped on the Sat Nav. 'Not one for another thirteen miles, Annie, I'm afraid.'

Martin winced. Anne hated to be called Annie.

'I can't wait that long, Martin. We'll have to stop.'

Marilyn placed a hand on Anne's knee. 'It's not a problem. The dogs could do with a leg stretch. I know I could.'

Bless you Marilyn, thought Martin. If only you knew you were the reason Anne wanted to stop. Marilyn was approaching fifty, but to her appearance was still everything. While Anne was content to scrape her hair back into a pony and walk around in a pair of leggings and scruffy trainers, Marilyn would venture nowhere unless she was immaculately presented. That included full make up and perfume. Lots of perfume. Far too much perfume according to Anne. Martin had to admit he hadn't noticed,

but it drove Anne mad and she devoted a lot of time and energy hinting to Marilyn to tone it down. When Marilyn missed Anne's not-so-subtle hints, she had stepped up her campaign to phase two: coughing theatrically the moment Marilyn sat beside her.

Today Anne had initially found relief in opening her window and angling her head to take in the air. After ten minutes Marilyn complained that she was cold.

Martin braced himself for Anne finally letting rip. 'Well, wear some clothes then instead of flashing your tits about the place like some kind of teenager.' To her credit, Anne said nothing. Anne never understood why women painted themselves like that because she was naturally beautiful. Even though time had done its best to break her body, thought Martin, it had yet to sour her looks. When she wasn't scowling.

A few minutes later Keith pulled into a layby.

Keith had barely declared 'pit stop,' before Anne was out of the car and taking great gulps of air.

Martin was glad Marilyn was too busy with the dogs to notice his wife's theatrics.

Marilyn and Keith's Springer Spaniel Milly squatted down.

'There you go, Anne,' said Marilyn. 'Good job we stopped as Milly was desperate for a pee.' She bent down and ruffled Milly's floppy ears. 'Good girl.'

Ben, Martin and Anne's Jack Russell Terrier, trotted over and added his contribution to Milly's deposit.

'And Ben, too!' cooed Marilyn. She turned to Anne. 'Don't you need to go, Anne love?'

Anne looked like she would burst a blood vessel at Marilyn's pleasantness and Martin tensed. Her fuse was shorter than it ever had been. He understood, she'd been through so much. Ever since her Tuboplasty all she did was run and go to the gym. She was supposed to be taking it easy, but Anne never did what she was told. It was one of the things he had loved most about her. *Did* love about her. She pushed herself to the limits. Part of him wondered if that was one of the reasons she couldn't conceive. He had read somewhere about Russian gymnasts not getting their period because they were so thin.

When they had started trying for a baby all those years ago, they were both heavy drinkers and overweight. The doctor advised them both that stopping the alcohol and trimming down would increase their chances of conceiving. Initially, they had thrown themselves into the

healthy lifestyle. The weight dropped off the pair of them in a few months and hopes were high. But when the baby still failed to appear, Martin lost hope. Then came the tests and the procedures. Hysterosalpingogram, Fimbrioplasty and the rest. Still nothing.

They had stopped having sex. Instead, the clinic provided them with alternative methods. He masturbated into a cup coated with a special solution purported to aid his sperm –- which were OK, just a little slow, apparently –- to find the egg. Once his part was over Anne would take his semen and squirt it into herself with a syringe and then spend the next hour standing on her head.

Martin felt he was part of a chemistry experiment rather than trying to father a child.

When the cup and handstands failed, they moved to IVF. The process made Martin feel even less involved in proceedings. They had his sperm all frozen and ready to go, so he saw no need to even be around. Feeling surplus to requirements, he slipped back into old habits. He would drink while away on business and eat burgers and onion rings and triple cooked chips. And when he got home, he'd feel so guilty it was almost as if he had cheated on her.

Not that she noticed. She was busy taking her temperatures and doing egg tests and God knew what. Anne had stopped walking him through the process months ago and he had stopped asking. This was Anne's problem. All he had to do was sign the cheques to the clinic.

When she wasn't marking off temperatures in a spreadsheet, she was at the gym. At first, he suspected her of having an affair, perhaps she had found a better sperm donor. After a shameful few weeks of snooping and following her, he was satisfied she just loved to run. Too much in his opinion. She had developed a six pack he found oddly off-putting. Not least of all because she officially had more muscles than him.

'I was feeling car sick.' The lie from his wife jolted Martin back to the present.

Marilyn's concern was genuine. 'Oh, you poor love. Is that why you needed the window open? I tell you what I'll get my coat from the boot so you can have the window open.'

Anne flashed the best smile she could muster for Marilyn. 'If you wouldn't mind, that would be great.'

Martin was ashamed by the relief he felt now his wife had gotten her own way. His hope Anne would see Marilyn as more than just 'glitz and tits' had taken a nose dive. He doubted the two would ever get on. Even though both he and Keith knew the effort Marilyn was putting into being amenable.

* * *

With a groan, Marilyn remembered she had packed her big coat at the bottom of the suitcase which was, as luck would have it, at the bottom of the luggage in the boot. All she had available was a short denim jacket with three-quarter sleeves which she couldn't button because of her boobs. Anyway, she hadn't bought it to be buttoned. Who buttoned denim jackets anyway?

Still, she'd said she would let Anne have the window open and Marilyn wasn't sure she could take another two hours of the woman's pronounced sighing and squirming. Honestly, why she had agreed to come in the first place she had no idea.

Marilyn loved Martin and the ever so smoochable Ben. Martin was funny and always had something nice to say. That was whenever Anne wasn't nearby. Martin's whole attitude changed for the worse whenever she was with him. He hardly ever spoke, just let her moan on and on about whatever it was she felt like moaning about at the time.

Her relationship with Anne started badly when she announced she and Keith had never wanted kids. All Anne ever talked about was IVF and ovulation. And in front of Keith. It had mortified Marilyn. You could share too much information. In all their years of marriage, Keith hadn't even seen her on the toilet.

Martin had looked apologetic and Keith was jiggling his leg the way he did when he was itching to walk out of somewhere. So Marilyn, being a natural peace-keeper had said, 'Oh, I don't think the boys want to hear about all our womanly stuff.' Anyone would have thought she had punched Anne in the face. The look she gave her was one of pure disgust. Yes, that was it. It disgusted her that she believed talking about your reproductive organs wasn't appropriate in the company of men.

Keith missed it, of course. He might have been a shrewd reader of business but when it came to women, he wasn't up to much. He was kind of sexist, she supposed, but it had never bothered her. She loved their life together and although he liked to think he was the boss and she was the little woman sometimes, he had only ever treated her like a princess.

Martin had saved the situation from escalating by pretending nothing had happened and saying it was time to go. He was such a dear man and been through so much.

Marilyn ignored what she suspected was a smug smile of victory on Anne's lips when she got back into the car. She had the window fully down and already Marilyn could feel her nipples hardening as the coastal wind found its way through her clothes. She pulled Milly close to her bosom and nuzzled her ear. 'You'll keep mummy warm won't you baby. Yes, you will,' she whispered.

Anne gave her a look and Marilyn wondered if she had overheard. So what if she had, things needed airing and the sooner they were out in the open the quicker they could move on. Or not.

Either way suited Marilyn just fine.

CHAPTER THREE

Pat Trainer didn't know how all this would end. She knew how she wanted it to end; she wanted it to end with her dancing on the corpses of the two animals that had murdered her husband and now pawed her daughter. The Simon one had done a good job of tying Pat to the chair and, as much as she struggled, her bonds would not loosen. They hadn't bothered to restrain Sally, and that alarmed Pat more than anything. They needed her free to move, and it was obvious why. Sally was sobbing, and her frightened eyes darted between her mother, the dead body of her father and her molesters.

Pat caught her daughter's eyes flit to the circular blade tucked into Simon's tracksuit bottoms. The knife that had killed her husband, and robbed Sally of a father.

The Simon one was too busy stroking Sally's auburn hair and rubbing his crotch to notice. Of the two he was the most repellent. He resembled a corpse in the early stages of decomposition. And when he had roughly grabbed her breasts and crotch earlier she discovered he smelled like one too.

'What's your name, pretty lady,' Simon asked Sally.

Sally turned to her mother for help. 'Mum?'

'Leave her alone,' snapped Pat.

Marc turned to Pat and gave her a look that chilled her to the core. 'Shut up you old slag or it'll be worse for you both.'

'She's only fourteen for God's sake.'

That caught Simon's attention. 'Fourteen? I ain't no paedo.'

It was almost comical to Pat how afraid he had become. As if being a murderer and rapist were perfectly fine but being a paedophile was abhorrent.

Marc gestured for Simon to calm down. He turned to Sally. 'Are you a virgin, darlin'?' he asked her with surprising tenderness.

Sally bubbled snot and nodded.

Simon became agitated further. Marc's hand cooled him again.

'Now, love, I know Mum's over there and you want to be your own girl and all that, but you have to tell me the truth. You know what's going to happen, you're a clever girl.'

Pat renewed her efforts to escape her bonds. 'If you touch her, I swear to God I will fucking kill you.'

Marc snapped at Simon to shut her up. Simon ran over and punched Pat in the face. He screamed something but Pat couldn't hear what it was. It was as if she had fallen into a pool of water. Her ears whined. Consciousness slipped away until she remembered where she was and what was happening and fought it. With a roar she gathered herself, driving away the creeping darkness.

Marc was still talking to Sally in soothing tones and her teary eyes were locked on his. She was nodding.

The whining in her ears subsided and Pat heard the conversation.

'...so, what do you say?'

She nodded again and a fresh tear rolled down her left cheek.

'Good girl. So, I'll ask you again. Are you a virgin?'

Sally shook her head.

'See,' declared Marc triumphantly. 'You ain't gonna be fucking no child. This pretty little thing is a woman now.'

To her surprise, Pat's first instinct was to scold her daughter. Instead, she told her she loved her.

'Well, that changes things don't it?' agreed Simon as he groped her breasts, his erection now pushing out through his tracksuit.

Jesus Christ, what could she do?

An idea. 'You don't want a child. You want a woman that knows her way round a cock.'

That caught both creature's attention.

Pat was thinking fast. 'You don't get a husband and daughter by being a prude. I'll suck you to heaven and back. You'll never get it as good as I can give.'

Simon snorted. 'Shuttup you old bitch.'

'Exactly. Yes, she might be sexually active, but I am sexually experienced. Sure, you can put your dick in her mouth but I can *suck your cock*.' She tried to make those last three words as alluring as she could.

Simon picked up on her emphasis. And even Marc appeared intrigued.

Simon stepped over to Pat and looked at her hair. Age had dulled her fiery auburn, but it was obviously appealing to the animal. She fixed him with the best 'fuck me eyes' she could muster. 'The carpet matches the drapes if you know what I mean?'

'Does it?'

'And I'm tight too. Older women do exercises to get our men off.'

That was enough for Simon. 'I want to fuck this one. Can we fuck this one? She's sexy.'

'Are you sure?' asked Marc as if addressing a child who had taken too long making his mind up in a sweet shop and had a history of changing his mind.

Simon nodded his head emphatically.

Marc sighed at Pat. 'You know if you try anything I will kill your daughter.'

Pat nodded. Marc eyed her with suspicion. 'Untie Mummy here, Si. I think I'll see if she's as good as she says she is.'

'Fucking hell, Marc. I was the one that spotted them. I was the one who done the dad. I should go first innit?'

'Just untie her.'

'For fuck's sake,' hissed Simon under his breath as he worked on the rope.

Pins and needles jabbed at her hands as soon as they were freed, and she massaged them gently. She needed them working.

'You wanna go first?' asked Marc.

'Too right, yeah.'

Marc snatched the rope from him. 'Be my guest.'

'Thanks, mate.'

'And give me the knife, then.'

Simon passed him the blade and Marc tucked it into his jeans.

Marc turned to Sally. 'We need to tie you up now seeing as you're not going to be partaking in our little party. Behave or your mum is going to be treated very badly.'

Sally looked at her mum as she undid the drawstring on Simon's shell bottoms. They made eye

32

contact and the nod she gave her daughter was almost imperceptible. She hoped she caught it.

She had.

Sally snatched the knife from Marc's belt and slashed at his chest. The blade cut through his T-shirt and drew blood.

At the same time, Pat yanked Simon's bottoms and underpants down to his knees and pushed him backwards. Simon fell, his erect penis flopping around comically. As Simon hit the ground Pat was on him scratching and punching with everything she had. Simon waved his hands wildly, trying to deflect her blows.

'Run!' Pat screamed to her daughter.

Sally froze. She held out the knife making small, nervous arcs intended to keep Marc at bay. It seemed to only amuse him. The commotion behind him of no importance. His eyes saw only his prey, his lips curled into a sneer.

Simon grabbed both of Pat's wrists and for a moment they looked as if they were enjoying a lover's embrace; Pat straddling him, both breathless, eyes locked.

The illusion was shattered when Simon screeched for Marc to get her off him.

Pat pulled her arms outward and lowered her head towards Simon's. For an absurd moment, he thought she would kiss him. Instead, she sunk her teeth into the soft flesh of his cheek. Simon wailed as hot agony exploded in his face. He released his grip on her hands and punched Pat in the side of her head, but she only bit deeper. Thrashing wildly, Simon rolled, and he was then on top of her. He gripped her head and tried to exert pressure, to pull her off. He couldn't do it. It took two more punches before she finally fell away dazed. He tried to stand but staggered and crashed into a nest of tables.

Sally's attention darted between her blood-soaked mother and Marc who was edging towards her, his hand outstretched, his grin widening, his eyes mocking her.

The knife trembled in her hand.

'Give me the knife,' said Marc.

'Fuck you!'

He took another step forward and repeated his demand.

'Mum?'

Pat was slowly coming to her senses. Her eyes were open, but it was clear to Sally that she was still dazed.

Marc lunged for the knife and Sally dropped it, falling backwards. He snatched it up and rammed the blade into her stomach. Sally's eyes went wide and her mouth formed a silent O. She didn't scream or even cry. It was as if she just stopped. She brought her hands up to the knife. Marc withdrew the blade and stabbed again. This time she made a terrible sound like she was trying to be sick but in reverse. Blood spread across her top and spilled out onto the floor.

'No!' cried Pat. She crawled at speed on her hands and knees towards her daughter. She had no plan. She just needed to go to her.

Marc was too quick for her. Just as she came into range, he straightened and lashed out with his foot. He caught her in the chin and she fell unconscious.

A heavy silence fell on the room.

'Look at what the cunt did to my face.' A bite-sized chunk of Simon's left cheek hung free just above the jawline in a flap. Every time he pushed it back into place it rewarded him with a fresh flash of pain before falling free again. He kicked the unconscious Pat in the ribs.

'Shut the fuck up and let me see.'

Simon obeyed while Marc examined the wound. 'That's going to need stitches,' he said. 'But you know we can't go to a hospital.'

'They always go to vets in the films so the cops can't trace it.'

'This isn't a film, mate. And we ain't got no money to pay a vet off.'

'Then what are we going to do?'

'Hold up a while,' he snapped. 'They might have some money about the place.'

'Yeah. A secret stash or something.'

It was unlikely, thought Marc. Worth a look all the same.

Sally was now making gargling noises as she choked on her own blood.

'You still got time to fuck the girl before she snuffs it.'

'Jeez, I don't think I could get a stiffy. My cheek's killing me.'

Marc moved over to Sally and unbuttoned her jeans. He dragged them from her legs without care and she moaned in pain. He pulled her knickers off and knocked her legs open with a foot so he could look between them.

'She's got a decent cunt,' he said and slipped a finger in her. 'Tight too. You sure?'

'Fucking right I'm sure. I need to get me face fixed.'

'It's not that bad,' he said. 'Go and wash the blood off.'

'It hurts.'

'Then get some paracetamol.'

'Paracetamol? I need some industrial strength morphine or something.'

Marc had stopped listening. Her cunt felt great against his fingers. Marc took off his top and pulled down his pants. He spat on his hand and rubbed it in the dying girl's crotch. 'Well I came here to fuck, so fuck is what I'm going to do.'

When he thrust into her, she coughed up fresh blood.

He slapped her face. 'Hey, hey. You keep that shit to yourself, OK? If you put me off my stroke them I'm gonna seriously hurt your mum OK. Just keep still. You've done this before, it's no big deal.'

37

Her eyes rolled back into her head. He slapped her back into consciousness. 'And if you die before I come, your mum'll *really* be the worse off for it. OK?'

No response.

He slapped her again. 'OK?'

She gurgled something. Marc took that as a yes and started up again.

* * *

Simon went into the kitchen. He was in no mood to watch Marc fuck the girl. His face throbbed and he felt like he would throw up. It was worse than that one time he had an abscess. He wadded up kitchen towel and held it to the wound. He hadn't looked at it yet. He knew it was bad and having it visually confirmed would have sent him into more of a panic. He needed to find plasters or something. Anything.

He struck lucky in the drawer below the sink. Under some tea-towels was a small first aid kit. Inside was the usual mix of small plasters and pins. Underneath the

smaller items he saw a big square patch with sticky sides. He removed it from the sterile wrapper and slapped it on his cheek. More pain. 'Fucking hell.'

It wouldn't replace stitches, but he hoped it would at least aid the healing process. He grabbed a strip of sticking plasters and moved into the hall where there was a mirror. He avoided his reflection, bracing himself.

In the other room it sounded like Marc was nearing the end of his fuck. He was making those funny grunting noises he always made when he was going to cum. Marc had all the luck. Simon hoped he could get it up to fuck the mum before they left. He had a thing for Mums and only picked the young girls because it was the done thing. Young girls were everywhere on the TV on magazines advertising everything all done up sexy like. They were getting younger and younger and loads of rich blokes got into trouble for fucking them. You weren't supposed to fancy mum's, not really. But he did. The pain flared again and sent the small flicker of desire slinking away.

Simon turned to inspect the damage.

It was bad.

The sight of himself in the mirror was shocking. The patch he had applied only moments before was already red. His chin and chest were soaked in blood. It stained his teeth like when he drank red alco pops. He was a right mess.

Shit. He peeled the patch from his cheek.

It's not too bad, he lied. Again, he tried to reset the flap of skin. Each time he nudged it into place the wound wept more blood. The flap would hold for a few seconds then come away again.

* * *

The girl was still alive when Simon returned to the living room. He was about to close her eyes when she blinked. 'She's still bloody going,' he said.

Marc was too busy watching his come drool out of her cunt to reply. The stuff mesmerised him like it always did.

Simon never understood the fascination. When he shot his muck, he wanted to forget about it, not stare at it

40

like it was the most interesting thing in the world. For some reason it made him feel sad.

The mum was still out cold. The sight of her prone body filled him with rage. The fucking bitch had torn a chunk out of him.

He took the rope and bound her hands together behind her back. 'Where's the rest of the rope?'

'How the fuck should I know? Did you even bring it?'

'Course I fucking brung it.'

'Then you should know where it is.'

He hadn't brought it. 'Shit. I forgot. Can you go and get it? I want to tie her up better.'

'Get it yourself, I'm knackered.'

'For fuck's sake, Marc, just get it for me. I can't go outside looking like this can I?'

'There's no-one about, you prick.'

'Don't call me that.'

'Call you what? *Prick?*'

'You know I hate it.'

'Take it easy shit for brains I'm only fucking with you.' He tucked himself away and stood. 'I'll get your precious rope.'

'Cheers mate.' He said and worked on removing the mum's jeans. They were those skinny type he thought looked good, but he'd hate to wear something so tight. Lads even wore them now, and they all looked proper tossers because it made their feet look enormous and their arses hang down. It was Adidas trackie bottoms for him or fuck all.

The woman was wearing kids knickers. They had a cartoon on them with the logo 'Little Miss Sunshine.' She was ancient, what was she doing with a pair of undies like that? He cut them away with the knife. She did have ginger pubs, she had been right about that. But she had a horrible pouty cunt, with big massive thick lips. He hated fannies like that. Turned his stomach.

'Here's your rope,' announced Marc.

Simon took it. 'Have you seen the state of her fanny?'

He looked. 'What's wrong with it?'

'Are you blind? Look at the lips on it. It's like a kebab that's got all the meat hanging out of it.'

'Behave. Some birds are like that aren't they.'

'So what. Doesn't mean I have to like it do I?'

42

'Look I'm hungry can we hurry this up and go and get something to eat?'

'Fuck that,' sneered Simon. 'I need to make this bitch suffer for what she done to me.'

'It's not that bad.'

'Fuck off. I need a doctor.'

'It's not that bad.'

'It is. I looked in a mirror, didn't I? Look like a zombie tried to eat me, don't I?'

Marc looked at his watch. 'We've been here ages already.'

'This won't take long.'

* * *

'There's something seriously wrong with you,' said Marc as he looked at the results of Simon's efforts. He knew things were going to be bad when Simon had emerged wearing an improvised smock made from bin bags.

But nothing like this.

It was like something out of a horror film. The ones where there was a mad serial killer. Until then Marc had never considered him and Simon serial killers. Sure, they killed a lot of people, fucked them up pretty bad, too. But that was just killing people. The scene before him was straight out of a nightmare. He realised now they were in fact genuine serial killers right out of a Hollywood scriptwriter's twisted imagination.

When Simon had sliced the first of the mum's labia off she had awoken screaming. The knickers stuffed into her mouth and secured with Sellotape muffled her agony. She bucked like she was insane and Marc had thought no cowboy could have stayed on her for longer than a few seconds before coming off. But Simon was sitting on her stomach as if she were not moving at all, watching the blood spurt from her wound.

Her arms were tied at the wrist and secured to the leg of the dining table. It moved under her struggle and for a moment Marc was sure she would pull the leg from the table. But it held. Her feet were bound at the ankle and secured to the leg of the sofa. Marc sat on the sofa to provide some added weight. The woman was stretched

between the two items of furniture like a human hammock.

The screaming died to a whimpering sob when he turned and showed her the removed labia. He dangled the severed skin as if trying to entice a kitten with a pilchard. She screwed her eyes shut, fat tears rolling out either side.

Simon rolled his eyes and returned to between her legs. He extended the remaining labial flap out with his thumb and forefinger. It took him several attempts. The labia were slick with blood and it kept slipping from his fingers and snapping back. When he finally succeeded in pulling them taught Marc noted they were quite big, almost two inches long, Marc guessed. The knife sliced through them with ease.

The mum bucked again and almost toppled Simon from her this time. He jumped off her, a frown creasing his brow.

He kicked her in her bloody cunt. 'Women pay good money for fanny tucks. I heard it on the news. You should be grateful this is free. Your fanny was fucking horrible. Fucking horrible. I done you a favour.'

Before he had started his impromptu vaginoplasty Simon had disappeared into the kitchen for several

45

minutes and returned with a *Bag for Life* filled with stuff. Simon rummaged in it now and produced a carton of grapefruit juice. Without warning he poured it onto her mutilated genitalia.

Marc thought the woman would have a brain aneurysm she was screaming so hard.

Simon was giggling like a boy who had scared a girl with a spider.

This time the screaming continued. The noise agitated Simon, and he told her to shut up. When she didn't, he started stomping her. When that had no effect he started stabbing. She stopped screaming then.

He stabbed and stabbed. Over and over. Each wound spurting blood as the knife pulled out only to plunge again and again. Soon the wounds crossed over each other and he was tearing pieces out of her with his hands. He was covered in gore.

Marc felt queasy. Not from the gore. He'd seen plenty of that. But from the realisation that Simon was getting worse. The girl in the woods popped into his mind. The pets.

CHAPTER FOUR

When the cottage finally came into view Keith understood how a dying man in the desert felt when he saw an oasis. The last hour of the journey had been interminable. Thankfully Anne had emptied her bladder sufficiently that no further toilet breaks were requested. All the passengers had fallen in to a drowsy silence when the initial excitement of the journey had faded. The silence suited him just fine. Martin, however, looked stressed. Keith felt bad for him. He knew Martin and Anne, while not exactly having problems, were having a tough time. A lot of couples would have fared much worse under similar circumstances.

The A road had split off into a dirt track with an uphill gradient of 30 percent. On the passenger side he saw thick woods, to the driver's side he saw lopsided fields that appeared, to his untrained eye, overgrown. The track was wide enough for a single car and not once did he see a

lay-by or an area to allow other vehicles to pass. He spent the whole climb expecting to encounter an angry tractor driver demanding he reverse his 'bloody tourist car' back down again.

The cottage was gorgeous though, he noted with relief. If the brochure had exaggerated its looks, and it had turned out to be a hovel, Keith imagined they would already be in the middle of an almighty row. If anything, the picture in the brochure hadn't done the place justice. It was huge, complete with the traditional white exterior that promised tourists a taste of country life. The front sported six small double-hung windows, and the aged oak door was framed by a cliched but oh so picturesque rose trellis. A waist-high stone wall bordered the property and its surrounding land. It was exactly how you would want a wall around a country cottage to look. The gardens were huge and well looked after, with rose beds, bird baths and a patio with garden furniture to the side where one could admire the view. It would take him a while to get used to not being plugged into anything. No Internet, no Wi-Fi. Not even a land line. His Samsung, always fully charged and ready for business, failed to present a single bar, only the dreaded red X to indicate a lack of signal. More

alarmingly the emergency calls only option refused to appear. It made him uneasy even though being off the grid was the whole point of the weekend. For him at least.

'Keithy,' squealed Marilyn. 'Look at the view!'

'It sure is something.' It was. Beyond the wall there was about a hundred yards of wild grassland that sloped down to what he imagined were cliffs and then there was nothing but open sea as far as the eye could see.

The view from the front was less impressive. Rows of trees and bushes that halted as if something commanded them not to grow any further. The cut-off was so neat Keith wondered how the owners had managed it.

Keith noted a smile play on Anne's face. That should take a load of Martin's shoulders.

Loud barking as the dogs, free at last, darted off into the woods, chasing strange and exciting scents.

'Do you think they'll be all right with the cliffs?' asked Marilyn.

Keith admitted it was a concern. Milly wasn't the smartest of mutts. He doubted she would jump off on her own accord, but she'd chase a ball or a rabbit over there to her doom in the blink of an eye.

'She'll be fine,' offered Martin. He turned to his wife, 'Nice, isn't it?'

'It's lovely,' she said.

Everyone was happy.

Or at least he would be when he had a few drinks down him.

* * *

The property was too close to the cliffs for Marilyn's liking. Milly would chase a leaf on a gust of wind over the edge given half the chance. For now, she decided to keep the dogs under close supervision.

Danger assessed, she needed to get a drink down Keith as soon as possible. The journey had been stressful for everyone but as the driver he was the one who felt it most. Annie could be a right misery sometimes. How she'd landed herself a cracker like Martin was anyone's guess. He was so funny and thoughtful. He deserved better. It was arrogant but Marylin often wished she could split herself in two and help Martin out. She realised his

51

marriage was not running smoothly. It was also clear a lot of the blame lay directly at Annie's footsteps. Marriage was a partnership. Martin had gone through the same heartache as his wife. There was no need to treat him so poorly. A little TLC went a long, long way in Marilyn's book.

Ben ran to her and jumped into her open arms, placing his paws on each of her ample breast as he often did. It would leave a mark, not that she cared. A dog's love was so wonderful, and she felt blessed to be the object of such affection. She couldn't abide people complaining when an affectionate dog got a bit of dirt on their precious clothes. True, Marylin liked to always look her best, but a dog didn't know that, did it?

Poor things.

Anne scolded her dog. 'Down, Ben. Bad boy.'

Marilyn laughed and kissed Ben on the snout and he responded with an enthusiastic lick. 'It's no bother, Annie. I love Ben,' she switched to what she called *Doggy Talk*. 'Don't I, yes I do, you handsome doggy. Do you love your Auntie Marylin? Yes, you do, oh yes you do!'

'Come here Ben,' she barked and when the dog didn't respond she jerked him away from 'Auntie Marilyn'

by his collar. Ben cowered as if he was going to be smacked.

Martin stepped forward. 'Take it easy, love,' he said to Anne. 'Marilyn doesn't mind.'

'Sorry, I shouldn't encourage him. I just love his silly face.'

'No bother,' said Martin.

Everybody except Martin saw the angry look Anne flashed towards her husband.

'Right,' said Keith, clapping his hands. 'We need to unpack the most important thing first.'

Marilyn scampered to the boot and pulled out a silver bag. 'I packed it last so it would be first out.'

'You are a wonderful woman,' said Keith and kissed her nose.

Marilyn squealed in delight. 'Well, the driver needs his fuel.'

'Well I'm not a driver for another few days. My work is done. I'm on holiday.'

'So you are. Go and pour yourself a large one while I empty the car,' said Martin.

'You sure?'

Martin answered for everyone. 'We've got this. Driving is tiring enough.'

'Who am I to argue,' he said, taking the bag from his wife and heading off to the cottage. The dogs, sensing somewhere new to discover, trotted after him.

Marilyn turned to Martin and made a soppy face. 'Aw, Ben and Milly love each other so much.'

'We're lucky they get along so well. Ben can be a right terror as you know.'

She did. Other walkers in the park gave Ben and Martin a wide berth, justifiably so. Ben snapped at dogs that came too close. Except Milly. It was as if Milly brought the best out of Ben. Not that he was a bad dog, no she wouldn't say that. But he was a grumpy dog. She supposed that was Anne's fault too. She had almost strangled the poor thing pulling him away like that.

Keith appeared in the doorway. 'It's even nicer inside. All mod cons.'

Marilyn grabbed a few smaller bags and trotted towards her husband. 'Ooh, let me see. I can't wait.'

* * *

'I guess that leaves the unloading to us, then,' said Anne.

'Just unpack our stuff if it bothers you.'

'It bothers me that it *doesn't* bother you.'

'Why would it? They got the cottage for free. They drove us here. Bloody hell, they didn't even take the petrol money I offered. Come on, we're onto a good thing here. Nice country air. New places for you to go running.'

Anne wondered if that was a dig at her, then chided herself for being horrible. It was plain he was trying so hard to make things perfect. Maybe that was why she was bucking against him. *Stop being a cow.* 'You're right,' she said. 'Let's get the stuff into the house and have a cup of tea.'

'Tea? You're on holiday. Join me in a beer?'

The thought made her stomach churn. Ever since she had cut out the booze for conceiving she barely thought about it. 'It's barely midday.'

'You never used to let that bother you?'

'I used to be fifteen stone, things have changed.'

'It's like you've forgotten how to enjoy yourself.'

'I haven't. It's just that I've put things behind me.'

'Such as?'

'Like early morning drinking and chips.'

'And me?'

'Jesus, Martin. Is that what you think?'

'Do you blame me?'

'I don't blame you for anything.' Anne wasn't sure that was strictly true.

Martin sighed and softened his voice. 'I'm not so sure. Sometimes I feel--'

Marilyn emerged from the cottage. 'Chop chop, you guys. Those bags won't carry themselves.'

The moment gone, Martin fixed his face into a smile and hauled a suitcase from the boot. 'One suitcase coming up.'

'One? Surely a big strong man could manage two?'

Annie inwardly rolled her eyes at Marilyn. If she carried on massaging Martin's ego he might think she was interested in him. She wondered if Martin secretly liked it.

When was the last time you said something nice to him?

She couldn't remember. What was that meme? Marriage is just asking each other what you need from the

shops until you die. Or what shall we have for tea? Or asking him to come in a cup because your temperature's right?

She watched as Martin rose to the bait and hauled two cases from the boot.

She shook her head with affection for the first time in what seemed like years and grabbed a case herself.

* * *

It had only been an hour and already Anne was desperate to get out of the cottage. It was nice enough, but she wanted to see what Langflorn had to offer. She was eager to pick out a good route for her early morning run. The thought of the wind in her hair and battling against new environments exited her. She loved running. She often fantasised she would never come back. She would keep on running as the song said, leaving fibroids and IVF and all that shit behind.

And Martin?

Everybody else was occupied. Martin was busy unpacking, Keith was relaxing after the drive, and Marilyn was in the bathroom putting on yet more make up in between doting on Keith to see if he needed anything.

Anne imagined it would be a heinous social *faux pas* if she tried to take the dogs out on her own or even, perish the thought, just slipped out for an hour to get her bearings. Martin would take it as a snub while Keith and Marilyn would see it as not being in the spirit of the weekend.

After much consideration, Anne realised her best hope of getting out would be Marilyn. Keith was not going to move now his job of driving was done. Martin would hopefully see her walking the dogs with Marilyn as an opportunity for the women to bond. It annoyed her how concerned he was they all got along.

At first she had thought they were swingers. Martin wouldn't say no to a shag with Marilyn; he practically drooled whenever he saw her. And let's face it, Martin only ever came into plastic tubs these days. She felt bad for him, but he had to understand; she felt even worse. Whenever she thought of herself she thought of pipes and wires and how everything was just so... fucked.

Yes, that was the word. Nothing in her worked and she lay on table after table while people prodded and probed and scraped and nothing worked like it should and Jesus she wished she was dead.

That was probably an overstatement. Yet it felt right. She was tired of crying in hospital toilets, of opening herself for men and women to rummage inside her. Tired of seeing slips of girls pushing prams while glued to their mobile phones.

Once or twice she had considered snatching a child.

She had watched a girl who couldn't have been any older than fifteen, smoking and texting without a care for the crying child in the buggy. No, the girl had been too interested in the latest tweet or text from some other overly fecund wretch. Anne's heart went out to the baby when the girl slipped into the Post Office leaving the bawling child outside.

Anne had loitered by the child, so desperate to pick it up and comfort it. Her car was so near. Fifty yards, maybe less.

She hadn't gone through with it. That day had been the closest she'd ever come. The girl was an unfit

mother and Anne would love the child more than the chain smoking, phone obsessed girl ever would.

Martin would not have gone for it. And it was the thought of his disapproval that had stopped her from snatching the child. She wanted it so bad she had initially thought 'Fuck him,' which wasn't the way for a wife to think about her husband. Not at all.

She'd had it all planned. She would go to a women's shelter and claim she was on the run from an abusive ex that beat her and had designs on the child.

The thought of how close she'd come to becoming a crazy barren woman/child snatcher chilled her still. What had she been thinking?

Anne found Marylin in the bathroom. 'Hey, there. Do you fancy taking the dogs for a wander?' Anne impressed herself by sounding upbeat. You had to be upbeat when speaking to Marilyn, Anne had learned early on.

Marilyn was nowhere near as stupid as she claimed to be, not by a long shot, and her optimism and positivity was often mistaken for a childish naivety. That had been Anne's initial mistake.

'Sounds great Anne, just let me finish putting me slap on.'

That bloody woman and her make-up. It was ridiculous. 'There's no need, we're only taking the dogs for a quick walk.'

Marilyn looked at Anne as if she were mad. 'Oh, Keith would do his nut if I didn't have my face on.'

That a man would 'do his nut' because his wife didn't have any make up on was ridiculous to Anne. 'Humph, it's your face, it's got nothing to do with him.'

Marilyn replied without moving her eyes from her reflection in the mirror 'In his line of work appearance is very important.'

'Exactly. His line of work.'

'We're a team.'

'Sometimes you can be so gullible. You're not a team. You're his pet.' Anne instantly regretted her words and wondered why she had voiced them. True, she believed them but she had more sense than to air them publicly. Clearly not.

Marilyn stopped what she was doing and turned to Anne. Her face was cold. She wasn't as angry as Anne had

rightly expected her to be, but there was no mistaking her annoyance. 'You have no idea what you're talking about.'

'Don't I?' Anne, never one to back down from a confrontation wasn't about to start now. Least of all with a woman like this.

'No. You don't. And I have no idea why I agreed to come on this trip with you.'

'You came because Keith wanted you to come and you're a good little girl.'

'I came because my husband needs to unwind and we both like the country and Martin.'

The significance was not lost on Anne. 'So, it's like that then.'

Marilyn sighed. 'It wasn't, initially, no. I was prepared to have a nice holiday with my husband and his friends. It now appears that that is not going to be how it is. I made every effort to be nice to you and this is how you speak to me.'

An apology formed on Anne's lips then she dismissed it, she was too stubborn. 'Well, don't blame me! It's not my fault our husbands are having a bromance is it?'

'Maybe if you made love to your husband once in a while he wouldn't need one.'

It was as if Marilyn had slapped her.

Marilyn realised she had gone too far. Only moments ago, she had chided someone for prying into her marriage and here she was crashing through someone else's like a bulldozer. 'I'm sorry.'

Anne was beyond consoling. 'Oh, don't mind me, dear. Let's all have a laugh at the dried up old woman who is so very mean to her sex starved husband. Never mind that I've had four miscarriages trying to give that blabbermouth lump a child and ruined my insides.' That wasn't strictly true. The number of miscarriages was accurate enough, but it was Anne who was pushing for the baby. Martin had let slip he was willing to accept they couldn't conceive, even going as far as to look into fostering and adoption.

Marilyn was fuming. 'If you must know, I had a hysterectomy at thirty-three. Then again, I don't go around discussing my womanly business to anyone who'd listen. You aren't the only woman to want a child and be unable to conceive, Annie. But you are the only woman I know of that treats her husband like garbage even though he's done

everything a man could do to give his wife a child even when that wife is as dry as a desert.'

Marilyn took a deep breath to calm herself. Anne was stunned into silence.

'Now, if you don't mind. I'm going to finish making myself look presentable for my husband *and myself.*'

To Anne's surprise Marilyn pushed her, albeit gently, out of the bathroom and closed the door.

Anne seethed with anger and regret. She'd been an utter monster.

Her pride surged back. Fuck this. I'm taking Ben for a walk and this weekend can fuck right off.

SIMON

The games started when he was just a toddler. His father long gone, he shared a single bed with his mother in a damp DHSS bedsit in Hanley. His mother was eighteen and already drank too much and was weighed down with antidepressants.

At night, she would pull her son onto her belly, positioning his head between her breasts, and set his legs astride her flabby belly. She never looked at him, never spoke, never kissed him. She turned her head away from him and rocked him to sleep. He liked the rocking. He liked the way the rocking grew faster and her heartbeat louder. Her breath would sound like she had been running. Then she would make a noise like she had hurt herself. Then she would push him off her and breathlessly bark he go to sleep.

As he grew, his body soon felt her hands working underneath him. The rubbing made his tummy go funny. It tickled him but in a strange way that didn't make him giggle. It reminded him of the way his tummy somersaulted when he went on the Big Dipper. It wasn't quite the same, though. This new feeling lasted longer than the momentary flip and made his spine tingle. His mother never touched him directly, not then. Instead he was aware she was touching herself and the rubbing was an accidental consequence of that. All the same it felt nice, and he was always sad when she pushed him off her. He loved the sound of her heartbeat in his ear. He knew he had been born from her tummy and as he listened to her beating heart, he imagined he was inside again.

The first time he responded she had been angry. She had felt his tiny penis poke into her stretch-marked flab and slapped his face. He was disgusting. She was his mother. What was he doing?

He had no answers. He wailed huge snotty apologies. She had made him sleep facing the wall.

Her anger lasted a few days. When the games began again he tried to stop himself from going bigger. When he failed, he feared the worst. But no slap came, no

admonishment. Not until she had made the pain noise did she finally push him off. He was glad. The tickling was nice but the longer he could listen to her heart beating the better.

Things changed when he grew too tall to straddle her belly. At first, she had kept her legs closed while she worked. Now his erect penis hampered her hands, so she opened her legs and positioned him between them. The warmth coming from between her legs made his penis grew even harder. He remained still listening to the heartbeat of the woman who was his entire world, listening as it quickened, enjoying the sensation but knowing the increase in speed meant the intimacy was soon to end.

Her free hand reached out and clutched his penis. He jerked, a hot prickly sensation running up the back of his neck, as she pulled him and guided him and suddenly the warmth intensified at his tip. Her hands moved around to his backside and pushed him down and his penis into her. He recognised the sensation, like when he pulled his foreskin back in the bath to clean underneath, only this was a hundred, no a million times more potent. When she tried to guide him back away from the warmth, he almost

cried out. He obeyed, mother always knew best, then she urged him forward again. The pleasure returned. It was not as potent as the first time but it was still better than he had ever felt in the bath. She repeated the process until he found his own rhythm.

He could feel something building inside him. Something more than the tickling, something that was going to be big. He felt the need to move faster. Then she pushed him off her.

It was like the times he dashed from the warm communal bathroom across the frigid halls back to the bedsit.

It confused him. His hands went to his penis. It was all sticky. Instinctively he grabbed himself and pulled back the foreskin. It rewarded him with a familiar sensation and the building within him continued.

Soon he felt an explosion of pleasure and he made a noise that sounded like the one his mother made when she rocked him to sleep.

Shame and panic griped him. He had wet the bed. Mum would be mad.

But mum wasn't mad.

She was rubbing herself and making noises of her own again.

He was ten years old.

CHAPTER SIX

'Where's Anne?'

Keith gave Martin a sheepish look. 'I think she and Marilyn had words.'

Although he had known it was coming, the fact it had finally happened caused him to blush. 'For fuck's sake.'

Keith shrugged. 'She's been through a lot.' The words came out perfunctory, reminding him the way people said 'sorry for your loss,' whenever they felt obliged to.

'What was said?'

'I heard shouting. Couldn't make out what was said.'

Martin could tell he was lying. 'I'm so sorry,' he said.

'It'll all blow over. At least whatever is causing the tension is out in the open.'

Martin wasn't so sure. 'Yeah,' he said and went to look for his wife.

He found Marilyn in the kitchen washing dishes. She jumped when he approached. 'The crockery was filthy. No dishwasher. I wouldn't be able to eat off anything unless I cleaned it first.'

'Do you need a hand?'

'Don't be silly, Marty. I need something to do.'

'Have you seen Anne?'

She stopped scrubbing for a moment. Then continued. 'She's taken Ben for a walk?'

'Is everything OK?'

She turned to face him. She was wearing washing up gloves, and she wiped the suds on her World's sexiest Chef apron. 'We had an argument.'

'What about?'

'I said some things I shouldn't have.'

That sounded ominous. 'Like what?'

She averted his eyes. 'I... she was right to be angry. But she drove me to it, Marty. I'm sorry if I've dropped you in it.'

'What did you say?'

She turned her back to him and carried on sloshing out cups. 'I just want to forget it. There are certain things that push my buttons, Martin, and Anne pushed them all. I shouldn't have snapped. I couldn't help it.'

He wanted to know how she had dropped him in it. Then he remembered he and Keith had come back from the pub one night and he had let slip they didn't have sex anymore. The look on Marilyn's face had been one of utter horror. He had regretted it instantly and supposed that was one of the things that turned Marilyn's attitude to Anne from tepid to downright cold.

Martin left her to the dishes and went out to the front of the cottage to see if he could work out where Anne had gone. It was unlikely she would have hiked back down the way they had come as there was nothing but fields. She might have ventured into the woods but they looked, to him at least, to be a difficult walk. Anne was stubborn, yes, but slow progress would have irritated her further. That meant she'd headed up the path to the left. It curved around the woods, riding upwards until the trees swallowed it up. The map of the area had detailed two

footpaths splitting off from that main path, both of which ended at the cliffs.

He set off in search of his wife.

* * *

Anne had been walking for twenty minutes and had yet to see another soul. At first she had relished the chance for some solitude, and besides you were never truly alone with a dog trotting at your side. Although she didn't class herself as an out-and-out townie, the isolation was already making her uneasy. She belonged in the city with all its conveniences. She didn't have it in her to move to a place like this. It was as if -- and this made her feel ridiculous for considering such nonsense -- that the place was annoyed that she was there. She was out of place in her Lycra running trousers and expensive pronation running shoes. The few times she had fantasised about 'getting away from it all' (as all people who lived in the city were wont to do from time to time) something hadn't quite clicked with her. Now she realised she hadn't been

fantasising about life in the country at all. It had been a life away from Martin. The realisation shocked and shamed her. He didn't deserve her scorn. She wondered if she still loved him. Their love had changed over time, as did most peoples, but was it so easy to simply fall out of love with someone? Was it that easy? Just like dropping her phone or tripping over his shoes in the hall?

No. It never was that easy. Nothing ever was. Not for her. She couldn't even get herself knocked up. All those times when she was younger and been late and she had prayed to God for her period to arrive. All that time wasted worrying. Life was too short.

Too short to waste a weekend with people she hardly knew. To waste with someone who wasn't in this with her anymore. It was her anger talking, and she knew it. They weren't wasted years. The last two were perhaps far from ideal, but wasted?

Then maybe you should try to fix it.

It was probably too late.

You won't know unless you try.

She didn't have the energy.

(or the inclination?)

No, that was unfair. She refused to believe she could just stop loving her husband like that. She refused to just give up.

Ben trotted over with a huge stick clamped between his teeth. It was so heavy his hind legs barely touched the floor.

For the first time in what seemed like forever, Anne smiled.

* * *

Anne's resolve evaporated when she saw Martin coming up the path towards her. She wondered if their lack of a sex life was the only thing he shared with Marilyn and Keith.

Ben paused and gazed at the approaching figure. When he realised, it was Martin the dog yapped off at speed. Martin dropped to his haunches and clapped his hands. When Ben reached him he jumped into his arms. The dog adored him. She enjoyed watching them together but today it failed to lift her mood. It seemed she was the

only one who had yet to renew her membership to his fan-club. Marilyn had obviously paid for the lifelong option.

'You never said you were going for a walk.'

The answer that came to her lips was 'I didn't think I had to seek your permission.' Instead she apologised.

'I was worried,' he added.

'There was no need. I just went for a walk.' She gestured around her. 'There nowhere for me to go.'

He ignored the complaint. 'It's beautiful, isn't it?'

'It's desolate.'

'Not the word I would have chosen but I see what you mean. We're not going to be able to pop to Waitrose for some mung beans are we?'

'When have we ever bought mung beans?' Why was she needling him so?

'You know what I mean. We're out in the sticks.'

'We are that,' she said.

Martin started down the hill. She followed.

'How's your face?' he asked. He never asked how she was feeling or if she was OK. It was always how's your face? It had been endearing ten years ago. Not anymore.

'It's fine.'

'Doesn't look fine to me.'

'It's not surprising when you hear that your husband's been discussing his sex life -- or lack of one -- with strangers.'

He stopped. 'What are you talking about?'

'Marilyn had the temerity to tell me I should fuck you more often.'

'Marilyn said that?'

'Of course she didn't. She said make love or some such bullshit. How dare you discuss that with strangers.'

'Firstly, I didn't. Secondly, they're hardly strangers. And thirdly, even if I did -- which I didn't -- how is it any different from you telling anyone who'll listen about our plumbing?'

'That's not the same thing.'

'How is it not?'

'It just is, Martin, and you know it is.'

'I bloody don't know it otherwise I wouldn't have asked, would I?'

'Then how does she know about our sex-life?'

'She knows about our *lack* of a sex life because I may have discussed it with Keith on a night out. It might come as a shock to you, but I sometimes would like to

deposit my sperm in you the normal way instead of a chemically treated cup!'

The venom in his voice made her flinch. Martin rarely raised his voice. His passion stirred the ghost of the warmth she used to feel for him.

'Men talk about these things just as much as women do. I confided in him and he must have told Marilyn.'

'I'm sure men do talk. It doesn't mean I have to like it.'

'For God's sake, Anne. It was a private conversation between two blokes in a pub. How was I supposed to know he'd go blabbering to Marilyn? Besides, you must have said something to provoke her. She's hardly likely to walk up to you and demand you sleep with your husband, is she?'

And there it was. In her indignation she had forgotten that she had pushed Marilyn into blurting it out. It still didn't excuse her, but it took the steam out of Anne's rising resentment. 'She's just so nice,' she said, exasperated.

The atmosphere cleared between them.

'She's harmless. Not a bad bone in her body.'

'You've looked then?'

'Course I have,' he answered without hesitation. 'But I love and want you, you grumpy cow.'

She smiled at that. They used to be so comfortable with each other. She used to call him stinky arse and laugh so hard at his jokes she thought she would die. And just for a moment everything was all right between them. A gust of sea air blew over them and she tasted the salt. 'Let's get back,' she said.

The couple set off down the hill, Ben trotting off ahead. When his hand sought hers, she took it without thinking and it felt good.

CHAPTER SEVEN

Simon waited in the car while Marc went to the shop. Marc had driven around looking for one of the big chain outlets for what seemed like hours.

'Big chains don't remember customers,' he had said.

'Yeah, but they've got CCTV and I'm in fucking agony.' The paracetamols were not touching the pain. He was swigging on a bottle of Bacardi he'd nicked from the fucking bitch's house. He hoped the alcohol would prevent an infection. They poured booze on bullet wounds and stuff in the films, so it must work.

Marc eventually returned. He tossed a small packet at Simon.

'Super glue? What the fuck are we going to do with super glue?'

'Don't you know nothing? Super glue was invented in Vietnam. They used it in the field to seal up bullet holes and shit.'

'No shit?' He wanted to believe.

'No shit.'

They stopped in a side road to apply it.

'It fucking burns,' complained Simon.

'Course it does. That's how you know it's working.'

'Jesus.'

'It's not that bad.'

'You said that before, you fucking liar.'

'It's not. The blood was making it look worse.' They had used the Bacardi and a tissue to clean the wound. 'It's even stopped bleeding.'

'Has it?'

'Yeah, mate. You're still an ugly fucker but the scar'll look good,' he lied. The scar would always be identifiable as a bite.

'We better lie low for a while,' said Simon. 'I need a breather.'

'All right.'

'Can we go to the beach? Sea air's supposed to be good for healing and that.'

'I dunno, the beach will be full of people, innit.'

Simon deflated. 'It doesn't have to be the beach. Just let's go near the sea.'

Marc took the map from the glove compartment and opened it. He roughly located their position. They weren't too far from the coast.

'Let me pick,' said Simon.

Marc handed him the map.

Simon put his finger to his lips as he scanned the map.

He jabbed his finger on the map. 'There!'

Marc leaned over. 'You sure?'

'I'm sure. Yes.'

Marc started the car. 'Langflorn it is then.'

* * *

'Enjoy your walk?' enquired Keith. He was on the way to being drunk. Anne counted four bottles of beer on the table.

Marilyn sat on the couch opposite him. Milly was curled on her lap and Marilyn played with her ears. Ben gave them both a sniff before trotting off and drinking noisily from the water bowl in the kitchen.

'Marilyn, can I have a word?' asked Anne.

She nodded for Marilyn to join her outside. Her heart was beating against her ribs she was so nervous. Apologising went against her natural stubbornness. Martin had leaned, over the course of their marriage, to find apologies in small gestures and looks on her part. She rarely came out and said the words. It was a childhood trait she had never outgrown.

Marilyn stepped out into the hall and closed the door. Her face held none of her usual cheeriness. Anne had never seen her look so cold.

Here goes. 'I wanted to apologise for what I said earlier.'

'Ok,' she replied coolly, hinting she expected more.

'It's no excuse, but I've been having a tough time and I took it out on you and I'm sorry.' The words came out in a rush and Anne worried they sounded insincere.

'I want to be friendly, Anne but you can't speak to me like that. And I can't speak to you like that either. I also apologise.'

Anne felt a weight lift from her. 'There's no need. It was all me.'

'Come here,' said Marilyn as she opened her arms to engulf Anne. Anne felt Marilyn's ample bosom press again her. She went with it, enjoying the gesture for a sign of peace. Once again, she choked on her perfume. 'I think I'm allergic to your perfume,' she said.

Marilyn looked horrified. 'You should have said. I've got others.' She leaned forward. 'To be honest, I'm not fond of this one myself,' she lowered her voice further, 'but Keith buys it me. I haven't the heart to tell him.'

They laughed.

* * *

Keith nodded to the sound of laughter from the other room. 'That's promising.'

Martin slumped in his chair and exhaled. 'Thank God,' he said. 'I think this weekend might work out after all.'

'More progress at your end?' He passed his friend a beer.

'I think so. As long as I don't mess it up.'

'The more you think about it, the greater chance you will.'

'You're such a wise old man,' smirked Martin.

'I'm only five years older than you, remember that. It'll pass you by in the blink of an eye.'

'A poet? As long as there's booze I think I'll be fine.'

They both raised their bottles. 'Let's drink to that,' said Keith.

And they did.

CHAPTER EIGHT

At least the water pressure was decent enough, thought Martin. The shower had coughed and spluttered when he turned it on but the water heated up quicker than expected. He wished Anne was in here with him. He had decided it was too early to push his luck. She would thaw in time. He had noticed the 'baby kit' in her suitcase so he was sure his services would be required over the weekend. She had packed the dreaded jar. There was no way he was wanking into that thing this weekend. She would have to let him contribute in the traditional manner. He had decided. He would put his foot down, and hopefully his dick in.

After Marilyn and Anne sorted things out they had all shared a drink. Anne had sipped a water. Small steps, he told himself. Keith had reminded them that not moving

from his chair for the rest of the day was his reward for driving, and that the youngsters should explore and leave him and Marilyn in peace. Marilyn agreed, providing they all walk down to the beach with the dogs in the morning. Martin was happy with that. He wanted time alone with his wife and he knew Anne was itching to see what Langflorn had to offer.

He stepped from the shower and wrapped a towel around his waist.

Anne was lying on the bed looking at printouts. Anne loved a printout. Whenever they were planning a trip, she always went online to investigate all the restaurants, pubs, B & B's and printed off prices and menus. She always knew what she was going to eat weeks in advance. Another thing Anne was fond of was super-sizing things: day trips often turned into overnight stays, or an overnight suddenly became a full weekend. He used to call her 'The Escalator.'

'I thought we could eat out. I checked out a couple of restaurants before we came. They seemed OK.'

She sounded much more optimistic. He risked a joke. 'There's a surprise,' he said.

'I like to be organised.' No hint of reproach but he was reminded of her charts and calendars. He dismissed them.

'So where are we going?'

'Have a look,' she offered him the papers.

'Ladies choice,' he said. His stomach growled. Beer on an empty stomach had been unwise. But you're on holiday, he reminded himself.

'OK, there's a pub called *The Coastguard*. Has rave reviews.'

'Great. I'm starving.'

'Good. It's a hike to the town, though. Might take forty-five minutes to an hour.'

'Well, a bit of fresh air never hurt anyone.' Besides, he doubted the locals went in for all that health crap she tried to make them both eat. His mind swam with juicy steaks and freshly caught seafood. A plate of Surf-n-turf would be just what the doctor ordered.

* * *

When Anne insisted Martin double check if Keith and Marilyn wanted to join them dining in the village he hoped they declined.

His heart sunk when he saw Marilyn's expression brighten at the prospect. Fortunately, it was Keith who answered.

'I'm a little tired, Martin. Besides, we've spent the best part of a day cooped up in the car together and I'm sure we'll be spending a lot of time in each other's company over the next couple of days. I fancy a nice, quiet, relaxing drink with my girls and taking in the view. And Ben of course.'

Ben's ear twitched at his name but he didn't move from his bed.

Good old Keith. 'You sure?'

This time it was Marilyn who answered. 'Absolutely. An evening with Keithy all to myself is my idea of an evening well spent.' She tipped her husband a wink before adding 'Not that spending time with the two of you would be time badly spent.'

Martin gave her a nod. 'I was going to say,' he laughed.

'Well, if you're sure,' said Anne, 'We'll be off then.'
She bent down to Ben who was snoring soundly and
patted his head. 'Be a good boy.' Ben opened his eyes,
looked at her with little interest and went back asleep.
'Charming.'

'Don't wait up,' said Martin.

'You youngsters have a good time,' said Keith. 'Us
old folks will enjoy a quiet night in.'

'Less of the old, you,' chastised Marilyn.

Martin looked at them both fondly.

* * *

The streets were too busy for Marc's liking.
Although not quite full summer holiday weather there
were enough people in shorts and skimpy skirts to give the
illusion. When he rolled down the window, the smell of
the sea rushed in to meet him and he heard gulls
squawking and wailing.

The sight and sounds perked Simon up.

'I want a ninety-niner.'

'If I see one I'll get you one. For fuck's sake.'

'There'll be loads of places selling them on the beach.'

'I told you we ain't going to the beach. It'll be chocka full of people and everyone's going to be gawping at the bloke with his face hanging off.'

Simon touched the wound in alarm. 'It's not hanging off is it? You said it wasn't that bad.' It hurt like it was very bad indeed.

'No. It's a figure of speech.'

'I'll put a plaster over it.'

Simon was never going to accept no for an answer. A gentle touch was needed.

'Look we can go along the coast. There will be loads of coves and shit, it'll be a laugh exploring them.' It was working. 'Besides, we need to get some new clothes. The bin bags caught the worst of it but we're still a bit ripe.'

'Where am I going to get a new trackie out here?'

'There'll be loads of shit like that out here. Walkers and stuff. We'll see if we can nick some from a shady little cottage. Places like this are full of them.'

'We might find one empty.'

'Maybe.'

'I've never been camping.'

'A cottage isn't camping.'

'Yeah, I know. But it's close though, innit? Being in nature with no lecky or tele.'

Marc suppressed a laugh. Simon was apt to throw a wobbler if he thought people were laughing at him. 'Nah, they'll have lecky and TV. Might not have a phone though. Deffo no internet or Wi-Fi.'

'Good for us.'

'Yup.'

'Alright. But I still wanna ice cream. It'll be good for the swelling.'

'Best put some on your balls then, you fucking animal.'

'Yeah, might need it. But I'm still horny.'

'Still?'

'Too right. You had all the fun with the girl.'

She was good. He was going to savour her memory. 'You'll just have to wait until we find someone else.'

They should lie low. That would be the sensible thing. But since when had they ever been sensible?

Experience told him that Simon would need to shoot his load into something soon or he'd start acting out, ruined cheek or not. Simon's violation of the mum only added more fuel to the fire.

He almost pitied the next poor cunt who found themselves caught up in it.

Almost.

MARC

'The thing to remember, son, is women aren't worth a shit.'

Marc's dad took a swig from the can of *Helden Brau* and offered it to his son. Marc took a sip although he found the taste bitter; it was expected of him.

'Attaboy,' his dad said. 'Put hairs on your chest.'

They were fishing in the local park. They never caught anything. His dad said the point wasn't to catch fish but to get out of the house and away from the little woman. Marc knew the little woman was his mother.

Marc was eleven years of age and overweight. It bothered his mother terribly. Marc hated it too because the kids at school called him fat and grabbed his boobs. Everyone laughed at him in the showers too. His dad was less bothered by his son's weight. He told Marc it was just

'puppy fat' and it would all turn to muscle when he got hairs on his dick. Marc didn't have hairs on his dick yet. A couple of his classmates had sprouted. He thought it looked stupid and was dreading the day his smooth skin was plagued by the short curly hair. When his dad explained that the hairs were a sign you had become a man, Marc changed his mind and started praying for them to arrive. Becoming a man meant the end of puppy fat and he would be like his dad who, to Marc, was the greatest man that ever lived.

'Women are spunk traps son. I think I've told you already.'

He had. You stuck your dick in a woman's hole and it felt good. They made stuff come out of you. If you weren't careful, that would be the end of you.

'So, they trick you into sticking your dick into them. They know all kinds of sneaky ways. They make you want to stick it in so bad that when you finally stick it in you ain't ever gonna pull it out again. Not even when all common sense tells you to.'

He didn't understand, and his dad caught the look. 'You'll know soon enough. You know how you like that girl at school, whatsername? Alice?'

Marc nodded.

'Well imagine that feeling you get when you see her but about a million times worse. It gets you so bad that you'll do anything for that feeling.'

Marc still didn't understand.

'Ever had a scab, and it feels good to itch it but your mum slaps you and tells you to leave it alone?'

He knew about that. Only last year he'd fallen off his bike and scraped his knees up badly.

'Well,' continued his dad, 'You know when you play with your dick...'

He blushed.

'Don't blush son. You play with that dick as much as you want. God gave you that dick and arms long enough to reach it, so it's all right with the Lord and nature.'

Marc had been doing it for years. Recently stuff shot out from his pee hole when the good feeling came. It was like runny snot. It tasted salty. He was sure it was spunk.

'Well when you put your dick in a woman, it feels just like that but better. Men go crazy chasing that feeling. Men will even pay money for it.

'But listen, I love your mother. And I am glad I have a son like you. But you've got to take what you want from a woman. Not the other way around. Don't let them trap you, son. They will trap you with their holes, and their words too if they can. There is always another hole to put your dick into. Never stick with one hole.'

'Did mum trap you?'

He considered this. 'Yes, she did. But I was lucky. When she stole my spunk, she gave me you in return. But I stopped her from stealing any more. I got the snip.' He made a gesture with two fingers like scissors closing.

'What's the snip?'

'It means she can steal my spunk all she wants but she can't make a baby with it.'

'I don't want to have a baby.'

'Good boy. Let them suck your dick or stick it in their arse.'

'In the bum?' Sometimes when he had a poo it felt nice. He sometimes wiped too much so his bum hole tingled. He wondered if it would feel good if he put his finger up there.

'Yeah, the shit pussy is just as good as the front. But wash your dick afterwards because it can get infected.'

'Like my scab when I picked it?'

'That's right.'

Marc checked and then pulled in his line. As he expected, it was empty. 'Dad?'

'What is it, son?'

'How do you make a girl suck your dick?'

'I think you're a bit too young for that. Give it a year or so. Girls make out that they don't like sex but guess what?'

'They're lying again?'

'Bingo. So, what you've got to do is persuade them.'

'How?'

'All women like a man to take control. Inside women are dirty.' He patted his chest and then tapped the side of his head. 'They have a need in them that makes them hot. Thing is, they have their brains all wired wrong. They think if they are forced to do dirty things they aren't dirty?'

'I don't get it.'

'Like see how your mum won't order chips from the chippy because she doesn't want to get fat?'

He nodded. His mum was a bit fat and dad called her a porker. Mum laughed but he didn't think she found it funny. Not really.

'But she'll eat mine and yours. You see in a woman's mind those chips won't make her fat because she didn't order them.'

Marc nodded his understanding even though he didn't.

'Women need you to make the decision for them. You *absolve* them of any responsibility. Do you know what absolve means?'

'Nope.'

'You see how you take a drink of my lager. The law says you can't drink legally until you're eighteen. I'm your dad and I say it's ok, so I absolve you from breaking the law. I make it not a crime.'

That made sense.

'So, when you get a girl interested and your dick gets hard, and she's all 'oh, no that's dirty' or 'I don't do that sort of thing' just make her suck it.'

'How?'

'Grab her head and push her mouth on it. Tell her you'll tell everyone she sucked it anyway or that you'll tell everyone she's frigid.'

'Frigid?'

'More crap. Women don't want people to know they had sex because they think everyone will call them bad names. At the same time, they don't want people to think they won't have sex because they'd call them frigid.'

'Damned if you do, damned if you don't.' It was one of his father's favourite sayings. Another was *Better out than in* after a burp, and *Who stood on that frog?* after a fart. Marc used them all whenever he could.

'You're a smart boy. Sometimes you might have to hurt them a little.' His voice became serious. 'But always remember to hit them where it doesn't show. Punch them in the stomach, son. Never the face. A good stomach punch will take all the fight out of a spunk trap. A punch to the face will leave a mark and she'll run off to her brother or dad or the police claiming all kinds of shit.'

His dad sometimes had to hit mum when she got out of line. When he was a baby seeing his mum get hit made him cry. Once dad explained it was part of marriage and women needed to be reminded of certain things he

understood. Mum was always so nice to dad and him afterwards Marc saw that his dad was right.

His dad crumpled up the can and burped.

'Better out than in,' they both said at the same time and laughed.

A short time later a woman Marc had never seen before came over and said hello to his dad. She was older than his dad and was wearing a lot of perfume that didn't quite hide the smell of booze. She was wearing dirty Reeboks with those funny socks that didn't cover her ankles. Her skirt was very short and from where he was sitting Marc could almost see her knickers. He would later find out that there were none to see. She sat on a bench.

'Now, I've got to talk to my friend a minute,' he said. 'Will you be ok?'

'Who is she dad?'

'Never you mind. And don't tell your mother you met her. Catch me a good big fish, eh?'

Marc agreed with a silent nod.

The woman stood when dad approached, and she tried to hold his hand. Dad slapped it away and pushed her towards the bushes. She stumbled and looked back at him like she was mad. Marc smiled when a raised finger from

his father sent her look packing and directed her in to the bushes.

Marc knew dad was going to do sex stuff. The only other reason people went into the bushes was to do a wee, and you always went on your own. Never in pairs. That was weird.

Marc hurried to the bushes, first checking there was nobody about to steal the rods (not that they were fantastic anyway).

A large tree stood in the clearing and various bushes formed a perimeter. It would have made an awesome den. Someone had snapped away the lower branches to make a clearing. It was a shame the place stank of cigarettes and wee. Cans and empty crisp packets were strewn all over the place.

The woman was squatting and at first Marc though she was having a wee and dad was watching. Marc shifted his position and saw the woman's head was moving back and forwards. It looked silly, like the way a chicken pecked at the ground. Then he saw she was sucking and licking his dad's dick like it was an ice lolly.

Dad's dick was massive. About a hundred times bigger than his. It looked redder, too. His was very pale

and thin and smooth. Dad's looked thick and rough. The woman seemed to like it though.

Dad was pulling her hair roughly. It looked like it hurt. She withdrew. 'Take it easy, Johno.'

He yanked her head roughly back, and her throat bent out at a funny angle the way it did when a vampire was preparing to feast on the blood of a victim. But he didn't bite her. 'Do you want a slap?'

Instead of being frightened and begging him not to hit her like mum did, she smiled. 'Do you wanna smack my arse?'

'I'll kick your arse.'

She stood up and hoisted her skirt. Marc saw the dark triangle of hair he knew was her fanny. He had never seen one before for real. Only in pictures.

His dad made a grab for her and she knocked his hand away. She moved to the tree and put her hands on the truck. She raised her bum in the air and pulled open her cheeks to show him her fanny.

Lads at school called a fanny a hole. It didn't look much like a hole to him. Marc thought her fanny looked sore. It was red and soggy. It made him feel sick, but he

couldn't take his eyes off it. Like whenever something scary was on TV but he was compelled to watch.

His dad's fingers disappeared inside her and she moaned. 'Give me the dick, daddy?'

'No talking bitch,' he snarled. He seemed mad. Then he stuck his dick in her fanny with a grunt and started moving.

Shortly his dad made another louder noise and moved away. He was out of breath. She remained with her hands on the tree while white stuff dripped from her fanny. His dad's spunk? It was like she was waiting for something else to happen.

'Clean yourself up,' his dad said. The woman squatted and weed the rest of the white stuff (spunk) out.

'Not bad,' said his dad. His dick was small now, and it glistened.

'There's someone out there,' said the woman.

His dad tucked himself away and cocked his head. 'Is that you Marc?'

Marc froze.

'Come out, son.'

Marc couldn't tell if he was angry or not. He did not move.

'Come out, son.'

Marc stepped into the clearing.

The woman stood and pulled down her skirt. She ground the deposit into the dirt with the toe of her dirty training shoe. 'Jesus, Johno your kid was watching us?'

'Were you watching, son?'

Marc nodded and looked at the woman from the corner of his eye.

His dad turned to the woman. 'Lift your skirt, Karen.'

'Piss off, Johno.'

'Fucking lift your skirt.'

'He's just a kid.'

'He ain't no kid, Karen. He's sixteen in a few days, aren't you son?'

He agreed with the lie. He looked even older than boys who were sixteen. He bought cigarettes with no problems.

'So, stop your whining and show him your goods.'

She hesitated.

'Do it.'

She rolled her eyes and hoisted the skirt, her own gaze cast heavenward while Marc roamed her exposed genitals.

'Like what you see, son?'

Marc wasn't sure. He nodded all the same.

'Do you want to touch it?'

Again, he wasn't sure.

She pulled down her skirt. 'I am not letting some kid touch my fanny, Johno.'

His dad stepped forward and used the low growl that Marc had heard him use on his mum. 'I swear to God if you pull that skirt down one more time without my say so, I'm gonna give you a fucking hiding to remember. *Comprende?*'

Marc liked the way *Comprende* sounded when his dad said it. He also liked the way women always did *comprende*.

'It's OK, dad,' he said. 'I don't want to touch it.'

His dad grabbed Karen by the throat and she made a pathetic strangled sound. 'Do you see what you fucking did. You've upset my son. He was just curious that's all. There was no need for you to act all stuck up.'

'I wasn't being stuck up, Johno love. I just thought--'

'No one wants to know what you thought. You've upset my son. Now you're gonna have to make it up to him, aren't you?'

She nodded. Her eyes were wide and brimmed with tears. Marc lacked the ability to articulate how her fear made him feel. His body did not and his penis twitched. Looking at Karen he was reminded of the way a dog flinched whenever he threatened to hit it. Hurting the dog was never the part he enjoyed the most. The cowering was what he craved. Hitting the dog was necessary to ensure it knew what you were capable of.

'What do you think we should do son?'

'I dunno dad.' All nervousness had gone. He was with his dad, and his dad was in charge.

'Should we make her suck your dick?'

Marc suddenly was overcome by a mixture of nausea, excitement and terror. It wasn't entirely unpleasant.

'Behave, Johno.'

'Did I tell you to say anything?'

'There is no way I'm--'

Marc didn't see the blow but when Karen fell to her knees, making those whooping noises his mum sometimes made, he knew what had happened.

'Get up, I hardly touched you.'

Karen rose, clutching her stomach.

'Get your dick out son.'

He hesitated.

'Don't be shy. Come on over. She wants to taste you, don't you Kaz?'

Her eyes pleaded with him.

Then his dad said something strange. 'I think I'll go for a pint with Scott tonight. Haven't seen him in ages. I've lots to tell him.'

'Johno, no.'

'Tell him you want to taste him.'

Karen beckoned him over. 'Come here, darling,' she said wiping away a tear.

As if in a trance he walked over. His legs felt heavy, and he thought he was going to fall over.

He stood before her, trembling.

She pulled down his zip and reached in for his penis. He gasped when she touched it.

It was too small to poke out from the zip and she unbuttoned his chinos. She looked at his dad for a moment. Marc recognised the look as the kind his mum gave him when he'd lied to her.

His dad gave her the look that said she had better not disobey him.

Then he was in her mouth. He couldn't believe it.

Her head started to make those chicken motions.

Then he came.

Karen spat out his semen. 'Bloody hell,'

His dad laughed. 'You were quick off the draw son. Don't worry, you'll last longer in the future. Karen's a wonder at cock sucking.' He kissed her gently on the brow. 'Thanks, baby. That means a lot to me. And the boy'll never forget it.'

But it wasn't quite true.

When Marc remembered that day, it was never Karen's lips around his tiny penis or him ejaculating inside of her that came to mind. It was always the fear in her eyes and how his dad's utter dominance had reduced her to something so utterly cowed and weak.

CHAPTER TEN

The sight and sounds of civilisation after not encountering another soul for the best part of an hour jarred Martin. They caught the town as people ending their working day mingled with tourists returning to their lodgings after a day of exploration and pottering. The streets thronged with an eclectic mix and Martin tried to guess who was local and who were merely visitors.

The walk to the town was comfortable enough. Martin had resisted the urge to hold her hand, but she had sought his a few hundred yards from the cottage. He wasted ten minutes wondering if the act was borne of habit or obligation or genuine affection before scolding himself that he was thinking too much into it. Now they were back in the real world he felt the need to indulge in small talk, which was out of character. Everything he

110

thought of sounded like the kind of thing he would say to a casual acquaintance rather than his wife.

As they sauntered along the street, they peered in the windows of closed touristy shops and perused the menus of pubs and restaurants. None of it was particularly inspiring.

'Have you noticed no matter where you are in the country these types of shops seem to sell the same tat?' She wasn't listening. 'With the exception of locally sourced tat.' He was babbling, trying to fill the silence with anything. Just like he had when they first met.

'Hmmm?' she said as she inspected a line of porcelain dogs.

Martin thought about asking Anne if she was OK. He wished he could somehow make a joke out of how sick and tired he was of asking her that. He said nothing.

She saw the look on his face, waved his concern away and said she was fine. He took her word for it even though he could feel the situation getting away from him again.

Martin checked himself. Don't ruin this before it has even got started. You're on a nice break with your wife

and you're about to have a nice meal. Or at least you hope it will be a nice meal. He also should stop saying nice.

The Coastguard looked great. It was a small, family owned affair but just the right side of fancy to put out-of-town customers accustomed to chains at ease. They were the only diners.

'This is nice, isn't it,' he said.

'I don't like being the only one's here,' she whispered.

He shared her discomfort. The portly waiter who had greeted them with threatening enthusiasm was staring at them from the bar. He wore a thick moustache twisted to thin curling points either end that reminded Martin of First World War era Germans. He kept picturing him wearing a monocle and spiked helmet combo.

'It'll pick up soon,' he said. Then added 'I hope.'

She pulled a face, and he smiled.

'Shall we ask Otto von Bismarck for some drinks?'

She slapped his hand. 'Shush, he'll hear you.'

He made a show of rubbing his hand. 'That's spousal abuse, you know?'

'Poor baby,' she said with mock sympathy.

'I'll get us some wine.'

'I'm fine. You go ahead.'

His disappointment was clear, and he expected her to scowl at him. 'I'm ovulating.'

'A glass won't hurt. You're on holiday.' He was pushing it.

'Oh, get a bottle of white then. I'll have *one* with you.'

Anne was on her second glass by the time the entrée arrived. She had surprised him by ordering garlic prawns when goat's cheese (an aid to fertility, apparently) was on the menu.

'Can we have another...?' he said to Bismarck, looking to his wife for approval. When she nodded for him to go ahead he finished, 'Bottle of white please.' He watched Anne as she swallowed down a prawn. 'Someone's found her appetite.'

She considered it. 'You know what?' she said. 'I am in a good mood.'

'I'm glad.' Don't push it, don't ruin it, don't say anything else.

'I'm sorry I've been difficult.'

Did she mean just today or lately? He took it to mean today.

'I know a weekend with Keith and Marilyn isn't the best holiday in the world--'

'No,' she interrupted. 'I don't just mean today, I mean lately. I get wrapped up in it all. I won't admit defeat, you know?'

He struggled to put his thoughts into words. 'We're not defeated. At least I don't think we are. I know it's your body, but I think that we have to consider other options.'

'I wasn't ready.'

'And now?'

'I'm not sure I will ever be ready.' She pushed her empty plate away. 'That was lovely.'

Martin finished his wine and poured another, she allowed him to fill her glass.

'There are so many stories out there, Martin. So many women who have tried longer than I have, who didn't give up, and then boom, it happened for them.'

It pained him that she said 'I' instead of 'we.' But he had stopped being part of the equation months ago. It was sperm plus egg equalled baby. Martin and Anne were no longer necessary. 'I ran out of steam,' he told her. 'And I'm sorry.'

She touched his hand. 'I became obsessed, still am. But it's fading. The realisation was setting in and I took it badly. I blamed you even though it was my body that let me down.'

'Don't say that.'

'You know it's true. When you brought the adoption literature, I felt like you'd turned your back on me, on us, on everything. I lost it. I'm not sure I've even found it again.'

'It sounds like you have.'

'That's the wine. I don't know if I can move on totally. Tomorrow I might be back to the miserable Annie you love so much.'

'I love you, whoever you are.' He said without thinking if it was actually true or not.

She took a big gulp of wine and poured herself another, took another gulp.

Martin braced himself for the bad news that was obviously coming.

'For a time I thought that I had fallen out of love with you. We had gone our separate ways. I'd lost myself in charts and temperatures and you'd turned back to your takeaway food and sneaky pints with Keith.' She stopped

his protest with a raised hand. 'It was my fault. I'd reduced you to nothing but a sperm donor, and for that I am truly sorry.'

'I don't blame you. You've been through so much. I don't know how you've stayed sane.'

'I'm not sure I have.' And that was true enough. But she had turned a corner. She didn't know how it had happened but since her walk alone earlier that day something had changed within her. She looked at the man sitting before her. This was not her husband, this was not a source of sperm; this was Martin. This was the man whose child she had desperately wanted to bear. No man had ever inspired that in her before. And she had become so entangled in her failure to do something millions of people managed to do accidentally that she had forgotten why she was trying to do it in the first place. The realisation of how close she had been to walking away from him was alarming.

'But I do love you, Martin. I do. And I'm so sorry.'

Martin was speechless. All the times he thought he would never hear those words from his wife again. They said them all the time when they left for work or before they hung up the phone but that was different. It had been

over a year since she had said it like that. He fought the urge to cry.

She saw his struggle and reached out and touched his cheek. 'Martin,' she said, was more apology than affection, and kissed him.

Martin choked back his emotion. He needed to lighten the mood or he would bawl like an infant. 'They weren't stingy with the garlic on those prawns, were they?' he wafted his hands before his nose.

She laughed. 'You have a knack for lowering the tone.'

'You said you love me, can't take it back now. And for the record. I have always loved you. From the moment I first saw you.'

'Really?'

'Well, from the moment I first saw your boobs.'

'Maybe you'll see them again tonight.'

Martin turned to Otto von Bismarck. 'More wine, please!'

Things were going to be all right from now on. He was sure of it.

* * *

The car had started misbehaving when they headed out of town for the coast. Whenever he pressed down on the accelerator, it made a lot of noise but returned little power. In higher gears it was less of an issue so he ignored it.

Simon was still complaining about not getting his ice-cream. The last thing he needed was a load of sugar. He had that agitated look that meant he was in the mood for something that might cause them problems. It had been a while since either of them had destroyed anyone as totally as Simon had destroyed the redhead. It would make the nationals, he was sure of it.

That was why he was heading away from civilisation. That was why he took the dirt track.

It had proven to be a bad idea.

Faced with the steep gradient Marc had shifted down to second and the engine made its displeasure clear.

'The car sounds funny,' said Simon. Thanks to the superglue and the cocktail of Bacardi and paracetamol the pain in his cheek had reduced to a dull throb.

'No shit Sherlock,' snapped Marc. Second gear was not providing enough power, and he shifted down to first. The engine roared. He knew fuck all about cars. He only really had films and TV to go on. That didn't stop him from recognising a bad noise when he heard one.

Fifty yards later the engine cut out, and the car started rolling back. He applied the hand brake and turned to Simon. 'That's it.'

'What'll we do now?'

'I suppose this track must go somewhere, innit. Let's suck it and see.'

'It looks dead steep.'

'The walk'll do us good. Nice sea air and all that. Like you said, good for your healing.'

'Yeah, I did, didn't I?' he said as if surprised he had said such a thing. 'I read that somewhere.'

'Me too,' said Marc.

'What about the motor?'

Marc shrugged. 'Leave the fucking thing, innit? No good to us now. Should have nicked a better one.'

'It was alright.' Simon had picked it.

For fuck's sake. 'You weren't to know, were you? Maybe we can find a jeep or a land rover up here. A good four-wheel-drive or something.'

'Yeah?'

'No danger. Come on.'

They set off up the track.

* * *

Keith rested his feet up on a spare chair and was happily sozzled. The view from the back patio was something else and made the troublesome journey worthwhile. His initial concerns at the public footpath running just outside their garden had washed way as he hadn't seen a soul in over an hour. Why people weren't walking through here constantly was beyond him. If only there was somewhere like this back home. You'd have to drag him away from it daily.

On his work travels he seized any opportunity to take a break at any parks or beauty spots he was fortunate enough drive through. Most people stopped at service

stations and the like for the Wi-Fi and a pee. His mobile managed most of the customer queries he received during the day and if they required prices he could call the office and one of the lads would help him out. Not that he needed any help. It was sad to admit, but he knew most of the codes and prices off by heart. He was always forgetting his brother's birthday yet knew the code for 5 litres of bleach. His priorities were all wrong, perhaps.

His most visited place was Victoria Park in Stafford city centre and he often stopped in the summer months for an ice-cream and a stroll along the river. It was his lucky place. He had finalised a £750,000 deal there while throwing crusts to ducks only last summer. When things were not going well, he often returned there to jump start himself. If driving to Stafford was too much of an inconvenience, he would take the A roads until something picturesque caught his eye. There was nothing like green open spaces to focus the mind. The directors tolerated his aversion to the office because he was making them money. His end-of-year bonus was always in the high five figure range.

Marilyn emerged from the cottage and Keith smiled at her. Most people took one look at his wife with

her make up and tan and blonde hair and jumped to the conclusion she was a bimbo gold digger. He made enough to support them both and had a decent chunk set away, but he was hardly a millionaire. It did concern him how she would react if the money were to dry up, not that it was going to. She did love her beauty treatments and shopping sprees. Marilyn had no job in the sense of working for an employer. She worked for Martin in a way. She kept the house spotless, his clothes were always clean and pressed, and a hot meal was always waiting for him. She also took care of any dinner parties or client entertaining in need of the family touch. A lot of his clients had been with him for years (Mac Brothers for thirty) and they were no longer interested in strip clubs or football matches like the younger clients. Marilyn always put on a bloody good show. Their relationship was an anachronism he admitted; the type of thing you saw on those sitcoms from the seventies like *The Good Life*. She was his Margot. And he wouldn't have changed it for the world.

* * *

Marilyn came out onto the patio with a bottle of white and two glasses. In each glass were three chilled grapes. It was a trick she'd learned to stop ice cubes diluting the wine, once the grapes had imparted their chill you simply ate them.

'Here we go darling. Not very chilled I'm afraid.'

'Well, it's a good job I am. Lovely isn't it?'

Marilyn smiled. She agreed the view was indeed lovely and took his hand. They gave each other a reassuring squeeze. She was so glad they had come. Keith badly needed a holiday. He worked far too hard. Most days he was up at 05:30 and straight on that bloody laptop, then out on the road until eight or nine o'clock at night. Then there were the days he stayed over in Derby or Birmingham. She used to worry he sought the comfort of others while away. His hunger for her on his return always sent such thoughts packing. Yes, she was glad to be here. Of course, they both would have preferred a beach holiday. Such things were impossible with her baby.

Pity about Martin and Anne being there too. Martin was a dear. He looked at her tits a bit too much for

her liking. Keith knew he did it but to him it was a compliment; you find my wife desirable, yes?

Anne was just so mean sometimes. She was constantly scowling and complaining at Martin. Keith told her that Martin had once confided in him he believed Anne resented him for the ruination of her body. That she only stayed with him because she was too afraid to be on her own.

Marilyn could see that. She might be physically fit and all that, but she made no effort to make herself look nice, always wore leggings and trainers and cut her hair short. Men didn't like that sort of thing. It was almost as if she wanted people to know how hurt she was on the inside just by looking at her. Then again, she told her gynaecological history to anyone that would listen so that wasn't true. She wondered how long their detente would last. She was prepared to move on, providing she kept her opinions to herself.

Milly chased a butterfly across the lawn while Ben watched. He was getting old now and was sitting in the shade, panting. Milly caught the butterfly in her mouth and turned to face her owners as if for guidance.

Marilyn raised her finger. 'Leave,' she said firmly.

Ben raised his ears at the command. Milly showed no reaction.

Marilyn repeated herself in a firmer tone.

Milly opened her mouth, and the butterfly flitted away. Milly flopped to the ground and rested her head on her paws, looking crestfallen.

'I like it when you're all domineering like that,' said Keith.

'Do you now? Then you had better be well behaved. I don't want any nonsense out of you or you'll be punished.'

He adopted a look of mock horror. 'But what if I'm bad?'

They had decided not to pack any of the paddles for fear Martin and Anne would hear. Their little game was far from kinky. But it was their game, their secret. Private. If others knew or suspected, then it would have lost much of what made it so fun.

The game took shape over the course of many years of Keith hinting at this and that and provoking slaps to his rear in a light-hearted manner. The first time she struck his buttocks in the bedroom he moaned and grew hard. She had been taken aback, and a little embarrassed,

when he explicitly asked her to spank him. The role had not come naturally to her. All her life she had been sexually submissive. She liked to surrender control to a lover. But her curiosity had outweighed her natural reticence and before she knew it she was strutting around the bedroom in suspenders and high heels scolding her husband for misbehaving and slapping a paddle in her hands. The power exhilarated her, and she was often as aroused as her husband.

He like to be put across her knee. She spanked him hard now, often leaving marks. Thorough thwacks replaced her initial timid strokes within the first few minutes as she felt his erection pressing into her legs. Sometimes he came on her knees. Such naughtiness earned him six more strokes and the task of licking her to orgasm as further punishment. If he managed to restrain himself and not come before she allowed him to, he could make love to her. His erections were always huge after a spanking and his lovemaking desperate and grateful.

They played the game perhaps four times a year. It took a lot out of Keith and she supposed that was the point. He was always so content in the afterglow. She wondered why he was that way. A lot of powerful men

liked that sort of thing she had heard. Politicians were always getting spanked, weren't they? He wasn't a politician, but he was 'powerful' in the business world. More to the point she wondered why she enjoyed it so much and what it said about her. She didn't masturbate often, but when she did, she always took the dominant role now.

'If you are bad, then you will have to be punished,' she said.

'What if I'm bad right now?'

'I'm not in the mood,' she said. This was also part of the game. The longer she made him wait the better it was for both of them. Already she felt the first dampening between her legs.

To take her mind off her growing arousal, she admired the view.

In the distance two figures cut through the fields and headed towards them.

CHAPTER ELEVEN

Keith didn't like the look of the two boys who approached one bit. They were in their early twenties and wore the dazed but smug expression a lot of youngsters sported these days. The skinny one had a big wound on his face. The squat, spotty one looked like he was borderline retarded. He realised he was being unkind. But after thirty years in sales you got the measure of a man -- or boy -- or you suffered for it.

'Alright?' said the spotty one. His accent wasn't local. Keith thought it Stoke or Derby. Swadlincote? Not as far as Nottingham though.

'Evening,' replied Keith.

The two youths exchanged an amused glance. 'Evening,' they responded in unison. A snigger.

'What you drinking?' asked Marc.

'Just some wine.'

'Can we have some?' asked Simon.

Of all the cheek. 'Unfortunately, there's only really enough for the two of us.'

'That's a bit rude,' said Simon

'Not really. We didn't plan on guests.'

'We don't wanna be your guests. We just wanna drink.'

'We have plenty of water or cordial, if you'd like?' offered Marilyn.

'What the fuck is cordial?' asked Simon.

Marc cuffed the back of his companion's head. 'God, you're a proper fucking idiot. She means juice. The stuff you add water to. Orange and that, right?' he looked to Marilyn for confirmation.

'That's right,' she said.

'But I want some booze.'

Keith stood. 'Look lads, it was nice chatting but I think my wife and I will bid you good night.' He turned to Marilyn. 'Shall we go inside, dear?'

Marc jumped over the wall. 'We haven't finished talking.'

Milly ran to the visitor, tail wagging. Marc crouched and patted her head.

'Listen here,' said Keith. 'We didn't invite you onto our property.'

'Invited myself, didn't I?'

'Then I'm afraid you'll have to un-invite yourself.'

'You hear that?' Marc called back to his companion. 'He's afraid.'

Simon scaled the wall. 'Ahh, bless him.'

'That is not what I meant. I would like you to leave now.'

Simon stood his ground. 'Make us.'

Marilyn called Milly to her.

Marc held the dog firm. 'I think she likes me.'

'Come to Mummy, Milly.'

'Silly old cow thinks she's its mum,' laughed Simon.

Keith took a step forward. Marilyn caught him by the elbow.

'Come to mummy, Milly,' she repeated.

Ben was standing now. Something was happening and he couldn't work it out.

Marc grabbed one of Milly's ears and dug his fingernails into her soft flesh. Milly yelped and tried to break free but Marc pinned her to the ground.

Ben barked.

'Leave her alone,' cried Marilyn.

Keith flushed with rage and stepped forward. 'You evil little bastard.'

Keith had experienced only one physical altercation in his life; thirteen years old arguing over something he couldn't recall with Kevin Brown. On that occasion things had not moved past the shoving and name calling stage. As an adult he had found himself in situations where he thought someone might attack him. A particularly intimidating youth had asked him the time one rainy October evening in Nottingham and he had braced himself for a mugging which never materialised. Ever since then he often considered how he would defend himself, wondered how he would deflect incoming blows and the best way to defeat his attacker. He had never thought it would be him doing the attacking. But here he was, striding towards a thug who was hurting a defenceless animal, fully intending to smash his face in.

When Simon lunged at him he realised television and films had not only failed to prepare him for actual combat, they had blatantly lied to him. The youth did not attack with a single punch but with a flurry of blows and kicks that overwhelmed Keith in a matter of seconds. The only action Keith could take was to cower and cover his face. The blows were relentless. Again and again Keith felt -- and heard -- each blow land against his head. A million miles away he could hear Ben barking and Marilyn screeching. He thought he heard the squat spotty youth laughing but he might have imagined it. Then an echoing darkness swallowed him.

* * *

When Keith fell to the ground Marilyn was sure the boy had killed him.

She wanted to move but her body refused to obey. She watched as the boy kicked the prone body of her husband, first in the ribs, then his head. He stamped on

his face until it was red with blood. Keith was no longer defending himself, his arms lay at his sides.

Marc released Milly and strode towards the barking Ben. He kicked the dog with such force it lifted from the ground. Marilyn heard a sickening crunch followed by an equally gut-wrenching yelp of agony from the terrier. Milly ran to her owner's feet and cowered. She was a good girl.

'Get her inside,' said Marc.

Marilyn felt drunk and half asleep. Something distracted her mind with all the wrong thoughts. Who will clear up the mess, I haven't eaten yet, she needed to check the lawn for dog mess. None of the important questions found their way into her consciousness.

Then she was in the house.

'Sit down,' a rough voice demanded.

She stared at the sofa as if it had suddenly appeared, unsure of what it was she was being asked to do.

Hands pushed down on her shoulders and she sat. She folded her hands on her lap and tried to remember why she had come to the living room and left Keith outside alone.

'Don't move.'

She didn't look at the voice. Instead she stared off into the distance with a puzzled look on her face.

* * *

Marc came into the room dragging Keith under the armpits behind him. 'Give us a hand then, fuck nuts.'

Simon grabbed the feet and lifted. 'Is he dead?'

'Pretty much.'

They dumped him over by the window. Milly ran to the body and licked his face.

'Gross,' said Simon.

'It's just a dog, she don't know no better.'

Simon took a step towards the dog.

'Leave it out, will you?'

'What?'

'You know what.'

'What the fuck do you care?'

'Look at the fucking state of it. It's hardly a Doberman is it?'

Milly was resting her head on Keith's chest. She shivered and whined.

'You killed the other thing.'

'That was a Terrier. They're nasty little fuckers. That,' he pointed at Milly, 'is a floppy eared excuse for a dog. Have a quick gander round the house. Make sure we're all locked up.'

'What for? We're in the middle of nowhere. I wanna play with the glamorous granny.'

'Because I said so, that's why.'

Mumbling under his breath, Simon closed the front door. He found the back door shut and locked. He decided against checking the windows as they were too small for anyone to get through without alerting them. He didn't bother checking upstairs.

'All locked. Can we start now?'

Marc took Marilyn by the chin and lifted her face to his. 'She's totally out of it.'

'Maybe she's drunk?'

'It's shock.'

'Who gives a fuck? Let's get her kit off.'

Marc slapped her face. Her cheek reddened, but she did not respond.

He slapped her again. 'Look at me,' he demanded. Slowly her eyes came into focus. 'There we go. What's your name, darling?'

'We need to find Keith,' she said.

'Must be the old bloke,' said Simon.

Marc spoke loudly and slowly as if explaining something to a deaf senile relative. 'Keith's dead, love. We kicked his fucking head in. See?'

He turned her head to show her what was left of her husband.

The sight of the body tore a scream from her and Marc punched her in the face and she fell back on the couch. She was dazed but clung to consciousness.

'Please don't hurt me,' she mumbled over and over like a prayer.

Simon noticed the almost imperceptible rise and fall of Keith's chest. 'He's still breathing,' he said, 'Give us the knife.'

Marc shook Marilyn until she regained lucidity. 'Your Keith is still with us, love. Would you like us to call an ambulance?'

'Please...'

'Please what, love? Please don't hurt you, please call an ambulance, please can I lend you a tenner? You need to be clearer.'

'Please...'

'She's lost it,' said Simon, and he stepped towards her. 'Shuttup.'

'Now, now, let the woman speak.' Marc grabbed her by the chin. 'Look at me.' He pulled out his knife, and she whimpered. The sound made him grow harder.

'Please help him.'

'She wants us to help him,' said Simon with a grin.

'You heard the lady, help the old geezer out,' he said as he handed the knife to Simon.

Simon got down on his knees behind Keith and lifted his head and shoulders onto his lap. Keith burbled blood from his lips. 'Hey love,' he called.

Marc pushed her head to see.

'I'll take good care of him for you and put him out of his misery.' He dragged the knife across his throat opening the soft flesh. Weakened pulses drooled instead of spurted. Keith made a faint gurgling sound, then died.

'That was a bit shit, wasn't it?'

'Certainly was,' agreed Marc.

Marilyn gave no indication she understood what had just happened.

'Now love, what are we going to do with you?'

'Don't hurt me.' She was crying now.

'Oh, we're going to hurt you. Just depends how much.'

Simon grinned. 'What will you do for us?'

'I--'

'What will you do for us?'

'I--.'

'Jesus, she's a fucking mong or something.'

'Listen love, we need to communicate here or things are going to be very bad.'

'Anything,' she said.

'Anything?'

She nodded.

'Like what? Make us a sandwich, do our washing?'

'Anything. Please don't hurt me?'

'So you said, darling. But you need to be more specific.'

A small voice replied, 'Sex stuff.'

'Sex stuff? I like the sound of that. What kind of sex stuff?'

Marilyn didn't answer. She didn't know what the right answer would be.

'Will you fuck us?'

She nodded.

'Ok then, show us what you've got.'

Dazed, Marilyn stood and stumbled over to Simon. She fell to her knees and her shaking fingers reached for his crotch. Simon slapped her hand away.

'What are you doing?'

'I – I,' she stammered.

'Take your fucking dress off and let's have a look at you, innit. We got to see if you're worth fucking.'

Her teary eyes darted from Simon to Marc. Nothing made sense and her body refused to obey her mind even as it screamed for her to do what they asked.

'Go on then,' said Marc.

She lifted her dress, revealing her Spanx.

'Stop,' shouted Simon and Marilyn froze, her dress stuck over her head.

'Jesus Christ, will you look at the state of those? Looks like a fucking nappy.'

'They're tummy tuckers, soft arse.'

'Oh, my God that's disgusting. Look at her legs.'

139

Marilyn trembled and the cellulite on her legs trembled with her.

'Don't be a prick,' said Marc. 'She's an old bird. As long as the minge is OK who gives a fuck. You don't look at the mantelpiece when you're poking the fire, do you?'

Marc walked over and pulled her pants aside and stuck a few fingers into her vagina.

Marilyn yelled.

'Jesus, you're shit out of luck here, mate. My fingers went straight in. Like a fucking yoghurt pot.'

Simon looked crestfallen. 'Here, let me have a go.'

When Simon rammed his fingers in Marilyn, she yelped again and resumed sobbing. Simon gave the dress a slap where he thought her head was. 'Shut your whining.' He jabbed his fingers in her again. 'You're right. We'll have to fuck her up the arse. I'm not going to get anything off that huge hole.'

Marc pulled the dress off Marilyn's head. 'Nice tits though,' he said. 'Maybe we could have a tit wank?'

'Take your bra off,' ordered Simon

Shivering, she obeyed and her large breasts fell free.

'Bit saggy,' the disappointment in Marc's voice obvious.

'Yeah but size is what matters. They're a good pair.' Simon gave her a wink. 'Nice tits, love.'

Marilyn nodded. She didn't know why.

'Get yer knickers off,' demanded Simon, he took his cock out and rubbed it.

Marc groaned. 'Does she have to? If it looks as bad as it feels it's going to be worse than a fucking run over hedgehog, all guts and no glory.'

'Well, I can hardly bum the bitch if she's got her belly warmers on, can I?'

'True enough.'

Simon returned his attention to the shivering Marilyn. 'Well, get them off then, you stupid bitch,' he roared and slapped her face to get his message across.

She stared at him. Simon slapped her a second time and again she stood there, shuddering.

'I think you broke her,' said Marc.

'Nah, she's just playing hard to get.' Simon punched Marilyn in the stomach and she sprayed vomit before falling to her knees, retching. Simon tuned to his partner. 'See I told you she was faking it.'

Marc laughed. 'She's puked on your trainees, mate.'

'Stupid cow, look what you've done.'

Marilyn was too busy being sick to hear. Simon grabbed a fistful of hair and yanked her head up. He spat in her face then head-butted her. He felt, rather than heard, her nose break. How he loved that feeling. It didn't bother him when some of her blood splashed his trainers.

Simon dragged Marilyn to the middle of the room and dumped her face down.

'Be careful smacking her too much, dickhead. If she dies I ain't fucking no corpse and if this hard on doesn't get a seeing to, then I'm gonna take it out on you,' warned Marc.

'Then tell her she needs to be more careful then.'

As Simon hoisted her up by her hips so he could yank down her knickers, mark bellowed in her ear: 'Be more fucking careful.' Then to Simon, 'Happy?'

Simon spread Marilyn's buttocks. 'Not a bad little arsehole. Looks pretty tight.' He spat on it and massaged it in with his thumb. He lined up the head of his penis and pushed. A brief resistance then he was inside her. He started pumping. 'Nice, indeed.'

Marilyn didn't make a sound. She was elsewhere.

CHAPTER TWELVE

It was almost dark by the time the cottage came into view. Martin was worse for the drink than Anne. She was pleasantly tiddly. Martin was plastered. For all his talk of making a deposit the natural way, Anne thought there was little chance of that now. It might be fun trying though. She couldn't explain her shift in attitude. It was as if she was a different person all of a sudden. All the resistance had drifted from her and she was enjoying the here and now. It might not follow her back home to the routine of daily life, but she had decided to hold on to it as long as she could. It was as if she were having a holiday romance. But with her husband.

Anne slowed when she saw that there were still wine glasses and an unfinished bottle on the patio furniture. Marilyn would have cleared them away. Perhaps

they took the opportunity of having the cottage to themselves for a bit of fun. Possible.

Then she saw there was litter on the lawn.

Not litter. A towel.

No.

It was Ben. Why was he sleeping outside?

Because he wasn't sleeping, was he?

Anne vaulted over the wall.

'What are you doing?' asked Martin. One minute his wife had been beside him, the next she was gone. He tried to raise his leg over the wall and staggered back. 'Hang on,' he said, 'I'm coming.'

Anne dropped to her knees. Ben was hardly breathing.

'Hey, boy. What's the matter?'

At the sound of her voice he opened his eyes and tried to raise his head. All he could manage was a barely audible whine.

Martin made it over the wall but landed on his arse. 'What's the matter?' he asked.

'It's Ben. He's sick?'

'Sick?'

She stroked his body and felt his ribs move in a way ribs should never move. Ben shivered.

'I think he's hurt.'

Martin appeared behind her. 'How?'

'That's what I'd like to know?'

'A wild animal?'

She shook her head. 'There's no blood. I think his ribs are broken.'

'Jesus,' hissed Martin. The news sobered him up. 'Do you think he was hit by a car or something?'

She tried to pick him up. The whine Ben made was so distressing she stopped.

'We need to get him to a vet.'

'We've had too much to drink?'

'Then the bloody vet can come to us. This is the countryside. There must be plenty of vets on call.'

'No phones.'

'Then we need to find something to carry him in. Why the fuck is he out here? Why haven't Keith or Marilyn done anything?'

That was a point. 'I'll go see,' said Martin.

'Hurry up,' she urged him. She turned to Ben and rubbed the tips of his ear between thumb and forefinger

just the way he liked. The familiar sensation caused him to try to sit up again. She held him gently in place. 'Hush baby.'

* * *

Martin was about to open the door when he heard a voice from inside the cottage. That in itself wasn't unusual. What was unusual was the voice belonged to neither of his friends. It was male and deep. Stranger still was what the voice was saying.

'Hurry up and come, you big fag.'

He stopped, cocked his head. It had to be the television. But it hadn't sounded like the television. It had sounded like someone in the front room of the cottage.

'It'll take me longer if you keep jabbering on and put me off me stroke.'

A different voice this time.

'I want to bum the old bitch,' said the first voice.

He waited for his alcohol addled brain to make sense of what he was hearing.

He moved to the window.

What he saw nearly caused him to wet himself.

Marilyn was on her knees. Her head was on the carpet. Her nose and mouth drooled blood and makeup was smeared across her face. From black mascara circles her blank, lachrymose eyes stared up at Martin, unseeing.

She was naked and a skinny man with a shaved head was violently fucking her. His face was a grimace of anger. Drool ran in a long strip from his lower lip to her back. His fingers tore at her fleshy hips leaving red marks. Beside them was a much stockier man. He was stroking his penis as he waited his turn.

Martin couldn't see Keith or Milly. There was enough blood about the place to suggest nothing good had come of either of them.

His instincts told him to run, but he had the presence of mind to retreat slowly into the shadows.

He crawled on his hands and knees to Anne.

'What are you doing?' she asked, as if he were fooling around.

'Keep your voice down,' he hissed.

'What is-'

'Shuttup. There's two men in the house. They're raping Marilyn.'

Anne looked at her husband as if he were delusional. 'What?'

'Listen to me. We need to get help or get a weapon or something. But we need to do it now.'

'You're serious?'

'Anne, stop fucking about. We need to help her. Now.'

'You are serious.'

'We need to move.'

'Did you see Keith?'

He shook his head. 'No. I think they might have killed him.'

'Oh my God.'

He looked round frantically, hoping to see something useful. His mind was not cooperating. All it did was replay the scene from the cottage. 'Think,' he said to himself. 'What can we use?'

'Let's just storm in there. We can catch them off guard.'

'They're a couple of psychopaths. We might take them but they might take us.' He didn't add that she would

most likely end up in the same position as Marilyn. 'We need a weapon.'

'The wine bottle,' she said and hurried to it.

It was a start. 'We need something more durable. The bottle might smash on the first hit. There must be something round the back. Gardening tools. Something.'

'I don't remember seeing a shed or anything.'

He took the bottle. 'Maybe you should run for help. You'll make it in what, twenty minutes?'

'No way I'm letting you go in there alone. You need all the help you can get. Two is better than one.'

He wasn't so sure. She was fit and had stamina but those men looked strong, vicious. 'This can't be happening.'

'I've an idea. I'll knock on the windows and get their attention. They'll come after me or at least one of them will. I should be able to outrun them.'

'No,' he said.

'Listen, this way there will only be one of them.'

'Unless there are more.'

'You said you saw two men.'

'But there could be more.'

'Let's work on the assumption that there are only two. We've no other choice. You will have to take on whoever remains in the house. Get Marilyn and Keith to the car and get out of there.'

'What about you?'

'I'll meet up with you when you're moving.'

'I don't like this.'

'Neither do I but we have to go now.'

'Just keep on running until you get to a phone. Don't come back.'

'No, listen. I'll try and lead him away and maybe I'll be able to cut back and we can defend ourselves from the cottage.' As she explained her plan she had to admit it wasn't a good one.

'No, just run. Get help. Keep it simple--'

'Stupid,' they finished together. That was it then. Decided. A plan. For what it was worth. 'Ready?'

'As I ever will be.'

She leaned forward and gave him a kiss. 'Good luck.'

Martin jogged over to the side of the cottage. The bottle felt strange in his hand. He had no doubt he would

use it. He just wasn't sure it would be effective. He waved to Anne.

Anne moved swiftly to the window. She kept below the glass. To get their attention, they had to see her. For them to see her she had to look in the window and that meant looking at the scene inside. She tried to imagine the worst thing she could. She thought about the scenes in *Death Wish 2* and *The Accused*.

None of them prepared her for what she saw.

The tears fell from her freely. She had never seen a human being look so destroyed as Marilyn. Not in real life. Her tears of anguish turned into tears of rage.

'Get off of her you dirty fuckers!'

The thin man who was raping Marilyn turned and looked at Anne. He wore an almost comical expression of surprise. 'Fuck,' he said.

The stocky man with bad skin bolted from the room.

Anne ran.

* * *

Martin waited in the shadows. His pulses throbbed and his heart rammed in his chest as if it wanted to escape. He tried to calm himself. Adrenaline was no good to him if he was a nervous wreck.

Anne's cry rang out into the night.

'Get off of her you dirty fuckers!'

He heard her running. He waited. He fought every ounce of common sense that told him to run too and held firm. The front door opened, and he heard heavier footsteps storm out into the night. He waited for the other man to follow. No one else came.

He slowly rounded the corner and stepped into the cottage. Everything looked different somehow, unreal even. He moved as slowly down the hall as his adrenaline would allow, trying not to make any noise. He heard someone talking.

'Your arse is pretty good for an old bird,' it said. The voice was casual, almost conversational.

The boy was behind Marilyn. He was stroking her buttocks and licking her rectum. With his free hand he wanked himself off.

Marilyn was perfectly still. Martin feared she was dead. Then he saw her chest move as her body automatically drew breath.

The room reeked of sex; the musky aroma of semen and sweat. And blood.

Then he saw Keith laying prostate beneath the window. His face was a mess of bruises and blood. His eyes were swollen shut, lips torn, cheeks split. If he was alive, then he needed medical aid immediately.

'It's tasty too. Even if it is an old one. You must look after yourself.'

This guy was certifiable. Keeping his disgust in check Martin crept forward. He planned to sneak close enough to brain the bastard with the bottle. It occurred to him he might kill the man. That was fine with him.

'I'd say,' the man paused while he tongued her rectum deeply. 'Yours is the nicest arse hole I've had. And I've had loads. Not bragging like. Even better than some young bird's ones.'

A few more steps and Martin would be in range.

The man ran his tongue down her cleft and sucked on Marilyn's labia. 'Tasty cunt, too.'

One step.

The floorboard creaked.

Simon snapped his head to the sound. Martin swung the bottle. Simon shifted his head, and the bottle glanced off his chin. It was enough to knock him off balance, but the momentum also forced Martin to topple forward. Martin fell to his hands and knees.

Simon stood, rubbing his chin.

Martin scrambled up, bottle in hand. This was not the plan, he said to himself.

The look on Simon's face was one of utter contempt. Martin knew then, even though he had a weapon, he was at a disadvantage. Martin was overweight and had been drinking. The man stood before him was younger, leaner and royally pissed off.

Simon launched himself at Martin.

CHAPTER THIRTEEN

Her calves were already burning. She had never run under the influence of alcohol before. She had hoped the adrenaline would clear her mind. It had, but only up to a point. She was not moving at her optimum speed.

He was faster than she had anticipated. He ran steadily and without a sound. She had been expecting him to scream obscenities after her, to threaten her. The silent determination of his pursuit was terrifying. He wasn't out to frighten her; he was out to catch her.

He was fifty yards away and gaining with every stride. Her plan of beating him to civilisation and summoning help was not looking good. Hopefully she had lured him far enough for Martin to help Marilyn. It was likely Martin was already dead. The thought tore at her and she felt herself weaken. She fought against it. No, he

would save them both and get Ben to a vet. *She* was the one who she needed to worry about.

She could hear him breathing now. Thunderous footsteps grew closer.

She needed to gain an advantage. He was faster and no doubt stronger.

Without thinking, she darted into the woodland.

And instantly regretted it. Low branches whipped her face, brushes and thorns clutched at her, her feet stumbled over stones and fallen twigs.

Keep an eye out for a branch that would be a good weapon.

Fat chance. The night, although clear, offered little light. She held little hope of losing him in the trees as her footsteps rang out like shotgun blasts on the undergrowth.

Her foot snagged on a root and she stumbled, her ankle twisted and hot pain flared. She ran through it. She would worry about it tomorrow. If she survived the night.

She needed to circle round and get back to the cottage. She risked a glance at her pursuer.

She couldn't see him. Or hear him.

She froze. Listening. The blood in her ears thumped and roared. She held her breath and her lungs

burned with the effort. Silence. She let it go and gasped for air.

A twig snapped to her left. Or was it to the right? The sound had too many surfaces to bounce off.

She patted the ground for something to defend herself with. Leaves, twigs, stones no larger than boiled sweets. Useless.

She held her breath again, annoyed that her own exhaustion was hampering her senses. She heard footsteps crunching, sweeping.

She tried to regulate her breathing. She needed to move. To run.

Another crack of undergrowth. Closer this time.

A foot caught her full in the face.

Her vision exploded in light. Then black.

* * *

'Cunt,' snarled Simon as he unleashed a flurry of blows. Martin had time to raise the bottle before it was knocked from his hand. It fell but didn't smash, and it

rolled away. The two men tumbled to the floor, Simon somehow managing to be on top of Martin.

The stench of the man assailed him; a cocktail of sweat and sex.

Martin tried to grab at the hands, but they were moving too fast.

Sweat dripped from Simon's brow and landed in Martin's left eye. The sensation enraged him and he roared, finding a fresh reserve of energy. Martin clawed at Simon's face. Simon knocked the attack away and grabbed at Martin's throat. 'I'll fucking kill you,' he spat, snot bubbling from his nose. Martin tried to pull the hands away, but it was as if they were made of iron. He feared those fingers would snap his neck if he didn't stop him. Already his vision was clouding as the oxygen supply to his brain was threatened.

Martin scratched at the wound on Simon's face. Simon howled but his grip did not loosen.

Black spots blotted the periphery of Martin's vision, and they multiplied swiftly until it was as if he was looking through a keyhole.

Not like this.

He was supposed to save them. His mind taunted him that he should have gone into the kitchen for a knife before coming in. The realisation of his stupidity temporarily overtook the realisation he was dying. He had failed his friends. Anne. Ben.

Then suddenly he could breathe. The pressure eased from his neck. He sucked in hot, painful air and retched.

A blurry image of Marilyn stood over him. She looked beautiful in soft focus like that, he thought. Slowly his vision cleared, and he saw the horrific reality. In her hand she held the broken wine bottle.

Martin sat up.

Simon was out cold, a trickle of blood on his brow.

Marilyn looked at the jagged edge of the bottle.

'Marilyn?'

She didn't reply. Her eyes remained transfixed on the bottle.

'Marilyn? We have to move.'

Marilyn crouched down beside the unconscious body of her rapist. She placed a hand on his cheek in an act that looked like compassion. Martin realised it was to

keep the head still as she drove the bottle deep into Simon's neck. Martin reached out as if to stop her and almost said 'no,' but it was too late. The jagged glass slid easily into the soft flesh. Martin had expected a lot of blood. Instead a small pool of blood formed around the glass where it punctured the skin.

Simon didn't wake up. Not even when she pulled the bottle out, a gout of blood finally spurting from the wound, and plunged it in again. And again. And again.

Martin moved then. He scooted over on his knees and steadied her hand. 'Easy,' he soothed. 'Easy. Let me have the bottle.' It was hard to look at her. Her eyes, once bright and clear, were red raw and almost puffed shut. Her face, usually so immaculately maintained, was bruised and swollen. All the times he had pictured her naked. He never imagined seeing that forbidden flesh so brutalised.

She released her grip and allowed him to take the bottle from her. Her eyes never moved from the blood drooling from the man that had so defiled her.

To Martin she was lost. He saw nothing in her blackened eyes. Nothing of the optimistic, ever cheery Marilyn from only a few hours before.

Martin fetched a throw from the sofa and draped it over her shoulders. She flinched at the contact but after a moment her shoulders relaxed almost imperceptibly as she drew the throw over her breasts.

He moved to Keith, already knowing what he would find, and felt for a pulse. He waited thirty seconds, a minute, but there was nothing. Keith was dead.

A whine from Milly acknowledged the fact.

Martin ran to the kitchen and grabbed the two biggest carving knives from the holder beside the cooker.

'Marilyn,' he said, trying to get her to stand. 'We need to get out of here. The other one is after Anne.'

It was as if he wasn't there.

'Marilyn!' he considered slapping her. Wasn't that the best way to cure shock? She probably wouldn't even feel it.

'I've got to go,' he said. He thrust a knife into her hand. With relief he felt her grip it.

'I'll be back.'

* * *

He had kicked her too hard. But the bitch had some legs on her, he'd give her that.

He took off her shoes and tossed them behind him. Then he dragged off her trousers and rolled her panties down her legs. Her cunt was hidden by the darkness. It didn't matter. This was about teaching her a lesson, not about sex. Bitch had interrupted his fun, bitch had made him run.

He spat on his cock to lubricate it. He slid into her easily, the sweat from her run aiding him.

It would be over quickly. Punishing women was the thing that got him off the best. All the other stuff was for Simon's benefit. This was all his. It was a shame she was unconscious. He would have loved to see the fear in her eyes. He pictured them wild and terrified, leaking tears. He heard her whimpering.

Incongruous girlish grunts escaped him as his orgasm grew closer. He shot his load deep inside her and shivered with pleasure. She was good. Shame Simon missed out on her. She was light enough for him to carry back to share. He thought about it then decided he

couldn't be bothered. Simon had bummed the granny anyway. Probably still was messing with her now.

He punched Anne in the face, feeling her nose break. He punched her again. Right, left, right. He stopped. There was no need to kill this one. He wanted her to live on. He wanted her to remember, to live in fear. He hoped he had ruined the cunt for life. That every time a man touched her she would shrink in fear as the ghost of him flared powerfully before her.

Shame it was too dark to watch his spunk leaking from her.

The sound of a car alarm bleeping and farting broke the silence.

He ran towards the sound.

* * *

Martin had a plan. It wasn't much of one, admittedly. It was a plan nonetheless.

He crouched in the shadows more scared than he had ever been in his life. He had barely survived his

encounter with the skinny one. The one who had chased after Anne was built like a brick shit house and here he was lying in wait for him. It was madness.

Surprise was his advantage. That and the knife. It felt good in his hands. It was heavy, quality. Not quite a chef's knife but a sturdy supermarket alternative.

You're rambling. Concentrate.

He had intended to get in the car and go for help. That was the logical thing to do. But Anne was out there somewhere. She was a good runner, she could have escaped. But he might have caught her. Might be doing to her what he had done to Marilyn and Keith.

Setting off the car alarm had seemed the best course of action. He hoped it would bring the man back to the house to investigate. And if the man was... and stop the man from hurting Anne if he had caught her.

Still, he battled with the instinct to run. He kept having to remind himself that running blindly into the dark was a very bad idea, even with the knife.

The longer he waited, the more uncertain he became. The plan was wrong, he should have run, he should have driven away, he shouldn't have left Marilyn. His blood was cooling. The weight of the knife was

bothering him now. It was a deadly weapon. He was planning murder. He was waiting in the dark for a man and was intending to stab him. To kill him. Six years ago he had killed a mouse with a shovel. The guilt remained to this day. But the mouse hadn't murdered his friend and raped his wife. He's probably raping Anne right now while you're hiding here like a tool worrying if you'll feel bad for killing him. Stop over thinking. It's kill or be killed. The realisation was surreal. People said such things all the time about the stupidest things like sports or business. He was saying it for real. He felt sick.

The car stopped beeping.

He was about to lean forward and give it a kick when he realised he was no longer alone.

* * *

Marc slowed as he neared the house. There was no sign of Simon. He thought he had perhaps set off the

alarm to get his attention and expected to see him standing by the car. He wasn't.

It was stupid of him to chase the woman, even though he had given it to her good when he caught her. Simon could look after himself. The old bloke was dead, and the woman was dead on the inside. He smiled at the way she'd said she'd do 'sex stuff.' Fucking hilarious. She'd done sex stuff alright. Got her arse tore up a storm stupid old cow. He wondered how much of her was left.

If that other bird hadn't turned up he might have had another bash at her. But they needed to get moving.

He stepped through the gate.

The alarm stopped.

The sudden silence put him on edge.

The front door was ajar.

'Si?'

No answer.

He moved to the window.

And saw Simon lying in a pool of blood. 'Shit.'

As he was about to run into the house, he caught movement in the reflection of the window. He turned expecting to see the woman he had left in the woods.

Instead he saw a man with a kitchen knife.

167

* * *

It was clear almost immediately Martin had made a mistake. Not only had he neglected to consider his approach would be reflected in the window, he soon realised he was holding the knife all wrong. Instead of holding it out from his body at stomach level for an easy thrust forward, he held it up above his head intending to strike down.

When the man turned, Martin hesitated, looking like a theatrical hack intending to assassinate Julius Caesar who had succumbed to stage fright.

In that second the man's hands flashed up and grabbed him by the wrist easily halting the intended strike.

Martin shifted his stance, but his move was anticipated, and the man pulled him off balance. They staggered away from the window and Martin was aware he had lost control of the knife even though he was wielding it. With a grin, the man twisted Martin's arm so the knife

was turned back against him. Martin realised with horror the man meant to plunge the blade into his chest.

The man's grin widened, the struggle apparently not requiring any effort on his part. Martin smacked his free hand against the man's face. The blow did nothing to distract him. He punched again. Harder this time.

The man laughed, actually laughed. He made a show of holding Martin's wrist with only his left hand. Martin used both hands to regain control of the blade. It made no difference.

The man laughed again. 'Pussy,' he said and landed a blow into Martin's ribs. The pain was instant and intense, and he let go of the knife. Martin knees buckled from under him and he tried to pull away, but the man held on to him and landed another blow.

'Pussy,' repeated the man. A third blow followed the taunt.

Martin couldn't breathe. It was as if his lungs had been filled with barbed wire. Bile scorched his throat.

His head was spinning and his vision blurred.

The man slammed his head into Martin's face. Everything exploded in white and Martin crumpled to the ground. Blood spurted from his broken nose soaking his

face. He was aware of neither fact. He was lying down and he was very tired and his ears were ringing. He knew he should try to get up, but he also knew he wouldn't be able to. So he thought he should just go to sleep. He was obviously much the worse for wear on the old drink and Anne would give him a lecture in the morning and probably do that trick of cooking something really stinky to make him feel worse like the time she...

He didn't feel the kick to the face that sent him to oblivion.

CHAPTER FOURTEEN

Marc gave the bloke an extra stamp on the face for good measure. Where the fuck had he come from? Fucked if he knew. Must have been with the bitch. Still he was out of commission now. The man's face was a bloody mess, lips split open to reveal broken teeth, eyes swollen shut. A faint wheezing moan whistled through his bloodied nostrils. Not quite dead. Marc stamped again on his head again. Cunt. The wheezing persisted. It didn't matter. Even if he regained consciousness (which he seriously doubted) he was no threat. Weak as a kitten he was. The things that passed for men these days made him wanna puke. Probably cried at films and talked about his feelings. Still he had *some* balls at least trying to shiv him like that.

Inside he saw Simon was dead. It had looked bad from the window, now he saw the full extent of his

injuries it was worse. Someone had gone to town on his throat. If he hadn't been looking at his corpse he would have thought Simon the prime suspect.

The grey-haired bloke was where they had dumped him. The dog was gone. And so was the glamorous granny.

He spotted a broken wine bottle stained with blood.

The soft prick with the knife had bigger balls than he first thought. He must have snuck up on Simon while he was busy fucking the granny. Shit that meant the granny was wandering free.

This was a right cluster fuck.

The granny wouldn't get far. She was ruined. Even if she hobbled her old legs down to the village it would be the best part of an hour before she even came across another person.

First he needed to move Simon. If he left him here it would only be a matter of time before the pigs linked Simon to him. True there was enough DNA at all their crime scenes to link them but so far they weren't on the database. Finding Simon would finally give them the starting point they needed.

How many had they done now? He only remembered the good ones. Must be twenty at least. A sense of loss drifted over him. It was at an end now. Nothing would be the same without Simon.

What now?

Sort Simon. Then look for the granny.

He went to the kitchen and grabbed some dish cloths and, after riffling through the cupboards, found a roll of bin bags. It was an arse ache they'd left the gaffa tape in the car. He sliced the power chords off the kettle and the toaster. It didn't need to be tight, just hold.

He wrapped the tea-towels around the ruins of Simon's throat.

'Sorry buddy,' he said. He didn't try to close his eyes. That shit only worked in films. Simon was always trying to close dead people's eyes. Maybe that's why he did the nipple thing? It pained him he would never have the chance to ask him. He was dead. He was a pain in the arse and a bit of a fuck-wit but there was no doubt in his mind that he was the best mate he'd ever had. Probably the only person he'd ever loved that wasn't family.

'No homo,' he said, when the genuine emotion embarrassed him.

He lifted up his head and covered it with the bin bag.

* * *

The bedroom was lit by a small bedside lamp.

Marilyn sat on the bed, arms folded, not looking at anything in particular. She must have come upstairs for something, but it had slipped her mind. She was crying silently. She did not sob or wail or shiver. Each tear rolled down her cheek and made a faint plopping sound as it hit the wooden floor.

She was naked. A blanket was draped over her shoulders. It smelled of dog.

Her body sang with pain. Her head, her nose, her ribs. Her bum.

Why did her bum hurt?

It also felt like she had fouled herself.

When she stood she saw there was blood and shit on the duvet.

Even if she bleached and boiled them the stain would never come out. They were ruined. She had ruined someone else's bedsheets, fouled them. With shit. The shame.

She would demand Keith drive her to the nearest M & S and purchase some replacements.

An image of Keith flashed in her mind. It was an unusual image. Not the one that usually popped up when she thought of him. He wasn't smiling, or on the bloody phone, or giving her that look when he'd been naughty.

This Keith was all swollen and red and split and cut and bleeding.

And dead.

She made a sound then. A sob that turned into a moan that grew into a wail.

She saw faces. Stupid leering evil faces.

They'd killed him. They'd kicked him to death and they'd...they'd...

Something licked her foot and she flinched.

Milly flinched, too.

'I'm sorry, sweetie. Mummy didn't mean to scare you.'

The dog wagged its tail and let out a whine.

Marilyn crouched down, the pain in her rectum flaring up, and petted her Milly. 'You're such a good girl,' she said.

Milly tilted her head. The praise was different somehow. The lack of emotion caused her to question the sentiment.

'Mummy's not feeling well.' She wanted Keith. Keith would look after her.

But Keith was dead. So was Ben. Little grumpy Ben.

Why had this happened? They were supposed to be on holiday.

Marilyn started to cry.

* * *

It took Anne too long to realise she was outside. It was dark, and she was cold. Next, she realised she was naked and she had a hell of a headache. Had she drank so much? It had gone down well enough, but Martin had polished off much more than she had. They'd been a bit

176

frisky on the way back. Maybe they'd nipped into the woods for a bit of alfresco loving.

Then where was her husband?

She sat up. Not totally naked. Her pants were missing. A stinging in her vagina. Shit.

Everything crashed into her at once.

Marilyn. Martin. Ben. Running through the woods. The men.

The man.

She knew then she had been raped.

He had caught her, and he had raped her. She could still feel his semen inside her.

A sob tried to force its way from her, but she refused to allow it.

Get up.

But he raped me. I've been raped.

Get up. Get your pants on.

Fuck you. I've been raped.

Stop whining. Get up. Get your pants on. The others need you.

She stood and searched for her knickers and pants. She automatically cupped her hand to keep the semen from leaking from her. It was a habit formed from trying

to keep Martin's inside her for as long as possible. She looked at it on her hand, the moonlight catching it. It looked no different from Martin's. She ran it through her fingers. It felt no different from his.

But it wasn't his. It was a rapist's. A psychopath rapist's come was inside her. She squatted down to push it out. Inserting her fingers and gently scraping it out as best she could. A douche, A douche, my kingdom for a douche.

Don't lose it, Anne.

She had no intention of losing it. Although she might not have a choice. People rarely, if ever, intentionally chose to lose their marbles.

Anne had always thought being raped was the worst thing that could happen to her. She had feared it and worried about it and once or twice thought it was going to happen. Now that it had all the feelings she thought she would experience were absent. She didn't feel ruined or violated (although she was certain those feelings most certainly would come) she felt enraged. Yes, that was the word. Enraged. Livid. She might have opened herself to a lot of attention in that area over the past few years. But she had let them, she hadn't liked it, but she had made

the decision. Yes, you may stick those ice-cold steel things up my fanny, Dr Samanuru. She had not given that squat scruffy bastard permission to stick his sweaty little dick in her. She had not. But he had gone and done it anyways. And that Enraged her. Enraged. And she trembled with the power of it.

Change of plan. She was no longer going to run for help. She was going to find him. And she was going to make him sorry.

She located her trousers by feeling the ground and slipped them on.

She wobbled, her legs suddenly unsteady and she sat down. The familiar tightness of lactic acid spread in her calves and she leaned against a tree to do her stretches. The routine offered her a semblance of normality although she seriously doubted anything would be normal again. Not for her, not for Marilyn.

You've got something in common with her now.

Jesus, did she ever let up?

The pain faded and she thought about Martin. He wasn't a fighter. Never been in a fight as far as she knew, not even in school.

Martin might be dead. He might be alive. Martinger's cat.

You're going to lose it.

'Shuttup,' she said and started jogging back to the cottage.

You're supposed to be going for help.

Yeah well, I'm not doing that now.

Yes, you're going to make a powerful, well-built young man sorry that he knocked you unconscious and raped you?

That's the plan.

How are you going to do that exactly?

She had no idea.

* * *

Marc was almost finished bagging his friend when he heard the wail from upstairs.

The silly cow was still in the house. Why? They might have missed a mobile. She might be on the phone now calling the police. 'Shitfire.'

He bolted up the stairs.

The wailing stopped when he reached the landing.

There were four doors, all closed. He listened for any other sounds.

The nearest door led to a bathroom. It was empty.

The second door revealed a bedroom. It had an empty suitcase and a wet towel on the bed. He saw running shoes and assumed they belonged to the bitch who had made him chase her. 'Slag,' he spat.

He knew he had the right room when he saw the stains on the bed.

Dirty old bitch hadn't even wiped herself.

The door to the en suite was open. It was empty.

He rolled his eyes. She was under the bed. How original. He would never have thought of looking there.

'Come out, love,' he said wearily. When he received no answer, he counted to three. 'I said get the fuck out of there, you stupid bitch. I haven't got time to be arsing about.'

He heard her moving about.

Marc dropped to his knees and lifted the duvet. He had intended to shout boo when he met the granny's frightened eyes.

Instead he was looking at a different set of eyes.

Milly barked.

That was when Marilyn burst from the wardrobe.

CHAPTER FIFTEEN

She knew he was dead as soon as she saw him lying there. He was flat on his back, mouth and eyes open, his face slick with blood.

Anne stood at the gate, not wanting to pass the threshold. If she stayed outside, then she could pretend Martin was still alive. If she went to him, she would know he was dead and she would have to deal with it.

But he was dead. There was no doubt. She knew if she ran to him and searched for a pulse or a sign of life, anything, she would find none. Her husband was dead.

She ran to him all the same.

She took his hand and rubbed it, willing the life into him. There was no pulse. She put her head to his chest and held her breath. All she could hear was her own

heartbeat thumping in her ears. She tapped his cheek and whispered his name.

Even as she felt for the pulse in his neck, she knew it was pointless.

He was dead.

'Martin,' she said.

There was no answer. He would never answer her again.

Then she heard a yelp coming from the house. Upstairs. A man's yelp. She ran to the door, intending to run towards the sound, then stopped herself.

Think.

She didn't know how many people were in the house. She didn't know if they were armed. She didn't know anything.

Fools rush in. Think.

She drew a blank.

Kitchen. Knives. Carefully.

She stepped into the hall, head darting left and right, eyes keened for an attacker. She poked her head into the living room, taking in the scene as best she could before snapping it back. She saw no one. No one living.

She peered in again and stayed. Keith was dead. No doubt. There was also a body wrapped in bin bags. She allowed herself a rueful smile. So Martin had taken one out.

She dashed to the kitchen for a knife. The block was almost empty. As an after thought she tucked a small steak knife into her trouser belt. She wasted a few seconds absurdly concerned about the safest place to conceal the knife. More sounds from upstairs sent her concerns packing.

It had to be Marilyn.

* * *

Marilyn brought the wire coat-hanger down with all her rage.

The thin metal struck his back with a satisfying thwack.

The man yelped in pain and arched his back.

Marilyn wasted no time in striking him again. And again.

The man raised an arm to ward off the blows and she whipped at his flesh. The man no longer yelped with each blow. His jaw set in a grim determination that told her she had made a mistake in attempting to take the offensive.

Marilyn stepped back as he rose and made a grab for the hangar. She should have run, should have found a better weapon. In a moment of lucidity her mind tormented her with the memory of Martin pressing a knife into her hands. Where the knife was now, she had no clue. The past few hours were nothing but a hazy fog. Every now and then an image would jump out at her only to be swallowed swiftly again. Bringing the wine to Keith on the patio. The men laughing at her underwear. Milly licking her. The knife.

A punch caught Marilyn on the cheek. The fog grew thicker and she felt herself being carried away on it like an angel on a cloud.

Some small part of her tried to fight it, knew if she allowed the fog to take her then it would be the last thing she ever did. Another part of her struggled to care. There was nothing left. And when strong hands wrapped around

her throat she found herself willing them to squeeze harder.

* * *

It took Anne less than a second to take in the scene. The maniac who had chased and raped her was on top of a naked and bloody Marilyn, his hands wrapped around her throat. His face twisted in a grimace as he choked the life from her. Her eyes bulged, her face an alarming purple.

The instinct to cry out for him to stop was strong but she ignored it. Alerting him to her presence would be a bad idea. Instead she strode towards the man and thrust the knife in his side. The blade hit a rib and didn't go in very far. She should have aimed lower, in the soft flesh of the stomach. She pulled the knife out and struck again but the man had moved. He staggered backwards, clutching his wound. With satisfaction Anne noticed blood seeping between his fingers. 'You fucking b-bitch,' he said.

Anne stood, legs apart, knife arm extended. 'That all you got to say to me, shithead?' The strength in her voice both shocked and impressed her. It had felt good to stick him. She wanted to do it again. It was probably a bad idea to bait him but she couldn't help herself.

The man looked at the blood on his hands. 'You're fucking dead,' he snarled.

'Come on then, shit head.'

She always detested the phrase *You go, girl!* But she internally screamed it to herself now.

Then she saw the man grin.

That's not good.

It wasn't. She had expected him to launch himself at her in a clumsy rage. She had visualised herself sidestepping his attack and slashing at him as he stumbled past her.

None of those things happened. The man snatched a pillow from the bed and held it out before him like a shield. The pillow was already covered in bloody hand prints.

Would he bleed out?

'Come back for more, have you darling?' he said.

The pain in her vagina reacted to his words. As did her rage. The anger had threatened to desert her when she saw his grin. His words acted like petrol on a dying ember.

'Can you get it up?'

What are you doing?

She had no answer for that.

'Don't you worry about me, darling. I'm always ready.'

And he was. She saw with a mixture of horror and revulsion a sizable erection straining at the crotch of his jeans. His face warned her this time he would ensure she was awake for the fun.

He was in range now and she took a step back. The determination was draining from her. Her mind working frantically to focus on defending herself and not the throbbing penis intent on raping her.

She might be able to push the knife through the pillow and into him but she would have to get in close. Every instinct told her that was a bad idea. That she should run.

The maniac shifted the pillow, gripping it by the corner and swiped at her hand. The pillow hit her with an

unexpected weight and the knife flew from her grip. She watched it clatter against the dresser dumbfounded.

The maniac was upon her. He gripped her shoulders and threw her against the dresser. Hard wooden angles jabbed into her spine, knocking the breath from her.

By the time she had composed herself he had hold of her pony tail and yanked her face to his sneering lips. She had never felt such fear in all her life.

He threw her face down on the bed and tore at her trousers.

For some unknown reason she was not moving. She was lying there motionless as if she was waiting for Martin to remove her pyjamas before sex.

What are you waiting for?

She rolled and lashed out with her foot, imagining it hitting him full in the face.

He caught it easily. That grin again.

'Now, that's not very nice is it?' he said.

She kicked with her free foot forcing him to deflect the blow.

'Get the fuck off me,' she heard herself say.

He twisted her foot and she yelped as the momentum turned her onto her front again.

This time she felt the knife jab in her belly.

She had forgotten all about it. She was amazed it was still there.

She felt her trousers slip over her buttocks.

Not again.

'Wait,' she shouted.

He ignored her. She heard him say something about tapping her ass this time.

Her hand went to the knife.

Quick. Once he gets on top of you that will be it.

She sensed him move away, presumably to remove his own trousers. She pictured his cocky grin as he took his time, relishing the power he had over this weak and terrified woman.

She turned. The knife drew blood as it sliced her stomach when she pulled it free, but she felt no pain.

The knife went in easily this time.

The maniac looked at her with what she could only describe as confusion.

His hands moved to the handle jutting out below his sternum. For a horrible moment she thought the grin

had returned, that he would pull the knife out and use it on her. But it wasn't a grin.

It was a grimace. A drool of blood leaked from his lips.

She kicked out with both feet and sent him back to the floor.

She stood, trousers and knickers at her knees, and watched him cough up more blood.

She hoisted up her trousers and tried to fasten them but the buttons were missing. She stood over the maniac.

He no longer looked like a maniac, a murderer, a rapist. He looked like a frightened boy who was about to die.

She pulled the knife from his chest, blood spurted.

She wanted to say something. Nothing came to mind. She was numb now. It was probably shock. Hot sweet tea was what she needed. So she had heard.

She pushed the knife into him again, slowly. Watching his eyes the whole time. They widened as the blade pierced his stomach and he let out a gasp and more blood.

There was resistance when she tried to pull the blade out again. It was funny the way it was easier to put it in than take it out.

Like his dick in you?

She stabbed him again. Eyes never leaving his.

A school teacher had tried to teach her a life lesson back in junior school. Mrs Donaldson had made the class of 2b squirt out tubes of toothpaste onto paper plates. They all had a lot of fun making the mess. But when Mrs Donaldson had told them to put the toothpaste back into the tubes they, understandably, had found it impossible. She couldn't remember what the point of it had been, although she was sure it had blown their pre-pubescent minds with its profundity. She simply recalled the memory. Thought of how stabbing the man who had raped her and killed her husband was somehow the reverse of the toothpaste exercise.

Again the knife proved harder to remove than insert. But she managed it. And slid it into his guts again.

And again.

She was still doing it when all life was gone from the maniac's eyes.

CHAPTER SIXTEEN

The steady beep of the heart monitor was the only sound when Anne entered the private room. Marilyn was awake, eyes staring at a muted TV screen.

Anne had been unable to rouse Marilyn that night and had taken the car and gone for help. When the paramedics arrived, Marilyn had suffered a heart attack. She was unconscious for thirty-six hours. Anne had prayed for Marilyn to give up, knowing that surviving, as she had, was not worth fighting for. But Marilyn had fought, had won, had survived. And now she was paying the price for her strength.

She was on a drip. Internal injuries were playing havoc with her digestion and she was still shitting blood.

Anne had gotten off lightly it seemed.

Marilyn wore her make-up. She still looked pale and her hair was what Martin used to call Bed head. But making the effort meant she was doing better. Not that Anne knew her that well. They had the bond of victims, but Anne refused to entertain the notion she was a victim. She was a survivor.

'How are you doing?' she asked, knowing how useless and insensitive the question. She had been asked the same question countless times and never could quite articulate precisely how she 'was doing.' Most people didn't really want you to answer, anyway. Everyday people asked colleagues and passing acquaintances (and sometimes close friends) how they were doing out of habit.

'I don't know,' she replied.

Anne supposed it was as good an answer as any.

'Do you know when you're going to be released?'

The twitch of a poorly mascara'd eye told Anne she hoped it wasn't any time soon. They hadn't talked about what happened to each other but the police had grilled them both pretty hard.

Apparently stabbing someone seventeen times wasn't strictly self-defence in the eyes of the law.

Reasonable force or some such bollocks. A sweaty woman with a bad perm and an ill-fitting green trouser suit was 'working diligently' to prove that the majority of the wounds were inflicted post mortem. Like Anne gave a shit.

'How are you doing, Annie?'

'Same as you, I think.'

'I can't remember killing the man. Simon.'

I can remember killing Marc well enough.

Simon Thomas and Marc Johnson. Linked to twenty-six murders and likely double that in sexual assaults. The newspapers were having a field day. Condemnation and horror, swiftly followed by a lurid interest in the pair's upbringing and sexual development. Then the strange cries for pity and sympathetic attempts to understand what made them what they were. It shamed her that she would have more than likely lapped up the coverage had she not been one of the victims.

That word again.

Victim. No. She was the Victor. She had beaten him.

They were throwing obscene amounts of money at her for Her Side of The Story. More than she earned in a year. Some idiot wanted her to write a book.

They'd double the money if she told them the latest development.

She had decisions to make. It should have been an easy one. It was proving anything but.

She kept telling herself it was her baby, not his.

Martin wouldn't want her to bring up Marc Johnson serial rapist slash murderer's baby, of that she was certain.

But something good had to come from all of this. Didn't it?

How the hell would I know?

AUTHOR'S NOTE

This was quite a departure for me. After my first novel *Personal Demons* I shifted from violent horror to more supernatural tales (albeit with equally horrifying, if less bloody, outcomes).

I still don't know where *Wrong Place Wrong Time* came from. If it was a movie it would be traumatic viewing (if it ever passed the censor), yet it almost wrote itself.

I was writing another novel alongside *WPWT* called *The Darkness Within*. It's about a young boy who thinks he has found the answer to all his problems but ends up gaining a whole lot more than he bargained for. That novel naturally settled into teen fiction while retaining the disturbing quality my work gravitates towards. Perhaps *WPWT* was born from that. Some part of me was horrified that I hadn't killed someone in a few hundred pages and overcompensated. I don't visit that part often. Maybe that's a good thing. Or maybe you prefer I went there more often…

Thanks for reading. See you next time.

https://www.facebook.com/TomStearnsHorror

Want more? Turn the page for the first chapter of

JENNA

Also available in paperback and Amazon kindle.

CHAPTER ONE

The phone vibrated through her pillow. Jenna never set an audible alarm in case it woke Hermione.

She gently pulled back the duvet and undressed. She raised her nightgown over her shoulders and dropped it on the bed. Next, she removed her knickers, then peeled off her woolly tights, then slipped out of the one-piece swimsuit. She stood in her final pair of knickers. They were faded, too tight, and had marked her flesh with angry red lines. She slipped them off and put on a fresh pair. Ones that fit better.

She folded the clothes neatly under her pillow and put on her school uniform before going downstairs to count the cans.

She hated the pleated skirt. Everyone wished it was shorter, and Penny and Chloe were always dreaming up ways to raise the hem. She longed to wear trousers. Not allowed. Her only option dark blue woollen tights.

Jenna's bra, faded grey, was a size too small and squashed her breasts. That suited her fine. She hated the things, the way everyone stared at them, always pawed them.

She made the mistake of asking Carrie for a sports bra one Christmas but only lezzers wear them and apparently that's worse than anything. Grimacing at the memory, she slipped on her steel-toed boots and tied the laces.

Fully dressed she gave herself a once over, avoiding eye contact as best she could. Her hair was getting longer, she could easily grab a handful. That was bad, needed to cut it again. School sent her home if it was too short. They suspended her for her first skinhead. She now had the balance just right; the teachers weren't pleased, but it was within acceptable boundaries.

She shifted the chest of drawers from the door as quietly as she could then went downstairs.

The man snoring on the couch was new to her, not one of the regulars. At least he was wearing clothes. He was overweight, and he cradled an empty bottle of Smart Price Bacardi between his breasts.

203

His beard, browned by tobacco, was crusted with food or more likely vomit. Empty cans lay on the carpet. Some were crushed, some intact. She counted nine. Special brew. Loose change was dotted amongst the cans and she pocketed £3.73. That would buy her a meal deal.

No sign of Carrie. She must have waddled up to bed. Miracle of miracles. Jenna put her hand on the seat of Carrie's armchair and grimaced when she felt the damp. She unzipped the cover. The cushion inside was wrapped in a bin bag, Jenna's idea, because the cushions never dried in time and Carrie kicked off if they weren't ready for the next nights session.

She counted twelve cans of cider and a half bottle of Smirnoff. She wondered where she had got the money for Smirnoff. No one paid for her any more and she'd been undisturbed last night. Must have nicked it. Or this mug had thought her worth it.

She threw the seat cover in the washing machine and set it to a time saver. They were out of washing powder, so she set it on a hot wash. She hoped it woke them up.

There were more cans on the kitchen table. Four Stella (must have been on offer) and two Carling. The

ashtray was piled high. She searched the nearby packets for any survivors but came up empty. A quick rummage through the ashtray rewarded her with two decent dog ends and she lit up the smaller of the two and put the other behind her ear before emptying the rest in the bin.

Someone had been sick in the sink. She ran the taps but needed to fish the chunks out with her fingers to get it down the plughole. She gagged. Must have been the bloke. Carrie might piss herself, but she never puked. Waste of booze.

No bleach, and the washing up detergent was empty. She unscrewed the top and filled it with water and shook up a few suds to clean Hermione's bowl.

Someone had discovered her stash of rice crispies. There was barely enough for a serving. She needed to get more. And milk. There went her meal deal.

She used water instead. Hermione wouldn't complain. None of them did. There was no-one to complain to.

* * *

The man in the living room started coughing, then fell into a heavy lung shredded hawk.

'Carrie?' he sounded like the rest of them. Hoarse, disorientated.

Jenna stood in the doorway. 'She's not here.'

'Oh, right. Giz a whiff of yer ciggie.'

She took a long, final drag down to the filter. 'All gone.'

He checked inside his B&H box and scrunched it in frustration when he found it empty. 'Have you got a ciggie, love?'

'No.'

'What's that behind yer ear, then?'

'Mine.'

'Jeez, yer a cold one. Help a fella out.'

'A quid.'

'A quid fer a dog end shit stick like that? Yer mad.'

'Seller's market.'

'You're Carrie's girl all right.'

Her face darkened and Bad Jenna wanted to rip the tongue from his mouth, to spit in his face, to rake her nails across her cheek. She shrugged instead.

'Go on give us the ciggie, I'm gasping.'

'Haven't you got a home to go to? You can't stay here.'

'I'm a guest.'

'I think you should leave.'

'I'll leave when Carrie tells me to.'

'She won't even remember who you are. I take it you bought the Smirnoff and the Stella? And she's in bed and you're on the couch. She'd suck off a dog for a brand name drink and you're on the couch. No, she won't know who the fuck you are.'

He stood up. 'You cheeky bitch.'

Jenna didn't flinch. 'Gonna hit me, are you? I've been battered by bigger men than you, more times than you've slept on couches of women who won't shag you.'

The slap rang out. It hurt more than expected. He hadn't looked much, but his palm had caught her just right.

She managed a snort. 'Make you feel better? Hitting a girl?'

He reconsidered, appeared repentant. She'd seen it before; an apology was brewing.

She held up a hand. 'Don't bother. You've had your fun, get out.'

He stood for a few swaying moments, then he did.

She angrily rubbed at her cheek, and her eyes welled with tears. Don't you dare. Don't you fucking dare. She raked a nail across the growing red splodge and a purple line formed. Better.

The sound of Hermione trotting to the toilet snapped her out of it and Jenna hurriedly started clearing up the remnants of the night before.

The place looked as presentable as it ever would when Hermione padded into the kitchen.

'Where's mum?'

'You know where she is. The same place she is every morning. In bed.'

'Oh,' she said and tucked into her cereal with water in silence. Jenna wet her hand under the tap and smoothed down her sister's hair. She paid her elder sister no attention.

Jenna returned to picking the mould off the last two slices of loaf. The crusts were riddled with it, but Hermione liked them cut off anyway. She smeared the ketchup as thick as she dared and sliced them into

triangles. Hermione loved triangles because she said it was posh. To her surprise there was a roll of foil in the drawer.

The sight of it reminded her of Todd. He was due a visit. That was never good. Not for anyone except Todd.

42975940R00127

Printed in Poland
by Amazon Fulfillment
Poland Sp. z o.o., Wrocław